Sophie

Kate Petty was born in 1951, the youngest
of four children. Her own teenage years were
spent at a coeducational boarding-school,
before going on to York University. She
divides her working life between publishing
and writing. She lives in London with her
husband and teenage son and daughter.

Sophie

KATE PETTY

Dolphin Paperbacks

These books are for Rachel, who approved.

First published in Great Britain in 1999
as a Dolphin paperback
by Orion Children's Books
a division of the Orion Publishing Group Ltd
Orion House
5 Upper St Martin's Lane
London WC2H 9EA

A catalogue record for this book is
available from the British Library

Typeset at The Spartan Press Ltd,
Lymington, Hants
Printed in Great Britain by
Clays Ltd, St Ives plc

ISBN 1 85881 656 4

One

Here we go again. Mum: Have you packed yet, Sophie? Me: Yeah. Mum: Have you left your room tidy? Me (lying): Yeah. Mum: Have you cleaned out your hamster? Me (knowing I can't get away with this): OK, OK, I'll clean her out . . . And so it goes on, Mum and Dad taking it in turns to get frantic until we're ready for off. I suppose I am looking forward to it really.

I still feel uncomfortable about Ben. Shouldn't do really; he is horribly immature. I don't know what he thinks I could see in him. I rang Hannah to talk about him, but there isn't much to say – except that he makes me feel bad. And I don't think she would understand – Hannah's great, but she hasn't had much experience with boys. I hope for her sake that the boys on her music course are more interesting than the sad loser we saw in Boots.

We always get up early the morning we go away. Traditionally Danny and I just fall into the car in our nightclothes and sleeping bags and carry on sleeping until we get to the boat. We used to dress inside our sleeping bags, but since we both wear T-shirts to sleep in these days it's just a question of adding shorts. It isn't as if the people on the boat are worth dressing up for. Travelling seems to take forever: five hours of fruit machines on the ferry and another five hours in a hot car driving on the wrong side of the road. One day my parents will think of some other way to get a suntan, something shocking like a package tour to Greece.

As soon as we're in France it's, 'Look Sophie – a chien!'

'Yes, Mother, it's a dog, wow.'

Or, 'Look Sophie, a cathedral/river/horses' or whatever.

'Mother, I'm not a kid. I don't have to have things pointed out for me.'

Ma looks crestfallen. Oh dear. I suppose it's because she gets excited by these things. Danny's almost as bad. 'Ball trap!' he reads; and then cackles. He does this every year. Even I know that ball trap is clay-pigeon shooting. He reads all the signposts in a Eurotrash accent. Every single one. Give me strength.

I know we're getting close when Mum just can't help starting up again – 'Look Sophie – sunflowers!' Admittedly there are great fields of the things, all busy turning their little faces to follow the sun, but – you know – see one field of sunflowers and you've seen them all. Mum doesn't seem to realise this. Every year she marvels all over again.

Dad concentrates on the driving, but even he seems to find France perennially wondrous. He positively encourages Danny. I can't understand how they manage to be so cheerful. I'm tired, hot, stiff, bored silly and bursting for a decent loo – not a hole in the ground, like the ones you find in roadside cafés.

At last we peel off the motorway. Ma and Pa squabble over the navigation of the last few turnings – perhaps they get tired too – and finally we're there, hauling up the road to the campsite and the manoir that goes with it. We park on the main drag, and pile out to book ourselves in and find our courier.

It's strange, this part. The campsite is humming – kids on bikes, people in swimsuits, olds playing boules, teenagers drifting about. All the activity takes place on a road that goes across the top. There's a bar, a shop, loos, showers, washing-up places, the office, table tennis, bike sheds, swimming-pool, all down this single highway. And that's where it all happens, with human traffic constantly passing backwards and forwards along it.

Like about a third of the people here, we're camping with a company called Suncampers. They lay on the tent and all the camping gear. It means you get the buzz of being under canvas – if you like that sort of thing, and the parents obviously do – without the hassle of carting all the stuff around. It's not even particularly cheap – you only have to look at all the posh cars to see the types who can afford it, but my ever-so-slightly Bohemian family seem to gain comfort from the fact that they're slumming it in a tent, rather than renting a gross 'caravilla'. Ho-hum. Personally, I usually try and chum up with someone in a caravilla as soon as possible. Better than a tent when it rains, I find.

Suncampers have their own couriers to meet and greet, usually gap-year kids and students. Quite funky sometimes. Certainly tanned and fit from spending all summer on a bicycle. I fell in love with a courier at this very campsite when I was about eight – only to be hopelessly disillusioned when I discovered that he had a girlfriend. To this day I can remember seeing them together for the first time – somewhere near the table tennis tables as I recall. I was grumpy for days – Mum and Dad still tease me about it!

We trooped over to the big green-and-yellow tent that served as the Suncampers office. There were posters and notices on a board outside and chairs and a brochure-covered table inside. We went in. Mum and Dad sat down. Danny and I hung around looking at the posters.

There were three couriers, two of them women. It took them a while to notice us because they were having a heated discussion about an awkward family who had just left. They spoke in English, so it was hard to pretend we hadn't overheard. My father coughed loudly and they all turned round together. One girl was the wholesome, friendly type, the other was the small bossy sort. The guy was the courier of your dreams – lean, tanned, short hair, white teeth. Very fit. He looked French, but he introduced himself in perfect public-school English. 'Hullo. I'm Jacy. You must be the Morris family. Sign in here with Coralie before I take you over to Reception, and then you can follow me to your tent.'

Mum was obviously about to tell him that we'd done this forever and knew the ropes, but I could see that she was charmed, and simply thanked him. Dad was already signing things for the lovely Coralie, with Danny close behind. I was left eyeballing the weasly girl, who wore a badge with the name Sonia. I couldn't think of anything to say, so went with Mum back to the car to get our passports for Reception. And then it was time to get back into the hot car and crawl along in low gear after Jacy on his bike.

'La Grange', as this campsite is called, is spread out over a large area. Parts of it are in a wood, others are on a slope that leads down to a lake, and there is the most recent 'prairie' (say it with a French accent), which is like a little suburbia of green-and-yellow Suncampers tents. The trees between the pitches haven't had a chance to grow yet, so I really hoped we'd be in the old, wooded bit, where you have shade and some privacy. I breathed a sigh of relief when Jacy's bike squealed to a halt and he hopped off at a pitch on the edge of the trees and unzipped the front of our huge tent, set up the sun umbrella over the table and righted the chairs that were leaning against it. He did this with a wonderful cat-like grace which had Mum and me mesmerised. Well, me anyhow.

So. Here was our home for the next two weeks. It had three bedrooms and a kitchen and a bit for sitting in if the weather was bad. The shower block and loos weren't too far away – nor were the bar, the shop, the restaurant and the swimming-pool. Good weather was almost guaranteed. Jacy swung back onto his bike and cycled off with a wave. I sat down in the car again. Mum gave a contented sigh. 'Isn't this great, Soph?'

Danny had been investigating the tent. 'I've chosen my pit. Coming for a walk round then, Soph? See if anything's changed?' Dan's amazing. We've been to this campsite God knows how many times and he can still get excited by a new boules pitch, or an extra flume in the swimming-pool.

'You go, Dan,' I said. 'I think I'll have a shower and sort my stuff out.'

'Suit yourself,' he said, but he looked a bit disappointed.

'Hire a bike if you want, Dan,' said Dad. 'Then you can chase the girls around!'

'Da-ad,' said Dan.

I humped my bag into my 'bedroom' and glumly contemplated the thought of two weeks under canvas with my un-cool brother, batty mum, and a dad who doesn't seem to realise that he stopped being God's gift to women at least twenty years ago.

Dan drew up with a screech and a skid outside our pitch – his campsite bike had very dodgy brakes. 'How long till supper?'

Mum, Dad and I had all showered and changed. Mum and Dad were transformed and raring to go. Even I felt a little less uncomfortable. I wore Levis to cover my white legs (well, white compared with people who hadn't just arrived) and a gauzy top with long sleeves. Another tradition – arrived at after years of Mum trying to cook for fractious children when she was knackered herself – is that we eat in the campsite crêperie the night we arrive. La Grange has quite a cool crêperie and tonight it was almost empty.

I had been quietly taking in the talent as we walked down the main drag, but most of the kids were small, and very probably Dutch – with white-blonde hair and brown legs. I peered into the bar as we went past, but that was pretty empty too.

'Did you see anyone our age on your travels, Dan?'

'Oh yes,' he said, as if it went without question. 'Loads. Looks quite lively.'

'Where've they all gone, then?'

'I dunno. Probably took one look at the gorgeous Sophie Morris and knew they couldn't compete, so they crawled away to die.'

'Thanks, Dan. So where are all the guys?'

'Fainted.'

'God you're so funny. There must be somewhere they all go in the evenings.' I didn't like not knowing, didn't like the thought of a scene that I wasn't part of.

'Don't worry,' said Dan. 'I'll sniff it out for us – no problem.'

'I'm not that bothered,' I said. 'It's always the same bunch of losers. Or French.'

'Heaven forbid that they should be French,' muttered Dad under his breath, but I chose not to hear him.

'You're so snooty, Sophie,' said Dan.

'Just because you like sad people,' I said, 'doesn't mean that I'm going to get thrilled about them.'

Then the waitress arrived with the menus.

I don't know why I felt quite so vehement, or why the prospect of the fortnight ahead filled me with such gloom. Perhaps it had to do with me and my friends promising to have holiday romances. Fat chance I stood if I couldn't even meet anyone! More probably it had something to do with the scene I'd left behind and all the business with Ben Southwell. I quite enjoy the sense of power I get when blokes fancy me, I suppose, but I hate it when they go all soppy and start talking about being in love with me. Nothing puts me off so quickly.

Brother Danny is the other problem, though he wouldn't know what I was talking about. He's so darned straight and honest and friendly and upfront – but he's never been the slightest bit cool. He doesn't care what trainers he wears or if his T-shirts have out-of-date bands on them. He even likes

classical music, for God's sake, and Abba! He just says, 'I like
it.' If I say, 'But only sad people like X – whatever,' he just
looks at me with that infuriating 'what's-the-big-deal' look of
his. He's like Mum, really, easily pleased. And this year, now
he's sixteen, things have changed a bit. He's still straight old
Dan, but with his new haircut he's actually quite good-looking.
Even Maddy's started batting her eyelashes at him. That's
another thing. My friends, who used to commiserate about the
awfulness of having an older brother who is grandma's pet,
teacher's pet etc., are now starting to insinuate that I'm lucky
to have an older brother! A different older brother, maybe, but
Dan!'

'OK sweetheart?' Dad hates me being silent. 'Pizza up to
scratch?'

'Fine,' I said.

'Another coke? Dan? We'll have another beer each, won't
we, chérie?' He beckoned to the waitress and ordered more
drinks for us all. She said, 'Bien sûr, Monsieur, tout de suite,'
and sashayed off in that way that French women have.

'Wow,' said Dad, the old lech. Mum slapped him on the
wrist and smiled indulgently.

'In your dreams,' she said.

'Mine, too,' said Dan wistfully.

'Never mind, bro,' I said.

The waitress reappeared. She looked like 'L'Arlésienne' (I've
been doing Van Gogh in art), all raven tresses and black eyes
with a perfect olive tanned skin. 'Merci,' said Dan as she
passed him his coke, and was rewarded with a wonderful slow,
full-lipped, white-toothed, sensuous smile.

'Concentrate on your food, chaps,' said Mum, catching my
eye.

We all fell into bed shortly after our meal. It was only half-
past ten our time, but eleven-thirty French time, and we had
been up since four-thirty. Needless to say, the lively bits of the
campsite were still humming – as if to taunt me.

Two

'Soph? Wake up, Soph. Dan's fetched the croissants and there's peaches for breakfast too.' I don't know why Mum gets so worked up. We have croissants from Tesco.

I grunted. 'It's too early.'

'Eleven o'clock French time '

'That's ten o'clock my time. Too early.'

Dan's voice. 'Come on Sophie. We can have a swim before it gets too crowded.'

Even less reason to get up. Half an hour later Mum unzipped my door. 'Mu-um!'

'Come on love. I want to put the breakfast stuff away, and Dad will eat your croissant if you don't claim it.'

'Oh all right.' I stumbled out into the extremely bright morning in my knickers and T-shirt and slumped into the chair nearest the hedge.

'Croissant. Eat.' Mum handed it to me and proceeded to wipe the table around me. I crammed it into my mouth, all flaky crumbs and buttery grease as Danny squealed round the corner into our pitch on his bike. Except it wasn't Dan. It was Jacy.

'Hi Mrs Morris! I've just come to check that everything's working and OK.'

Oh no. Not when I'm looking like this. I decided to stay sitting. He couldn't know I was in yesterday's knickers. Bits of my croissant had fallen onto the ground by the hedge. Suddenly I saw a tiny fieldmouse shoot out of the hedge and grab a large crumb. Now I don't mind small animals – I have a hamster after all – but this one scuttled so fast, I screamed and leapt up from my chair. 'Eeek!'

Mum and Jacy looked at me. 'What's up, Soph?'

I felt very stupid. 'A mouse,' I said lamely, tugging at my T-shirt and not knowing where to put myself as I stood there, white-legged.

'It's only a fieldmouse,' said Mum, smiling at Jacy.

Jacy looked at me coolly. 'It's when you have bare feet,' he said. 'You're afraid they're going to run right up your legs.'

'I'm going to wash,' I said, and dived into the tent. It was bad enough standing there half-dressed, but the way Jacy looked at me, I felt as if I hadn't got any clothes on at all. I could hear Mum and Jacy in the kitchen bit of the tent. The cooker was different from last time and we hadn't quite sussed it out. I prayed that they wouldn't get any closer. They went outside again and Jacy got on his bike. 'There's not a lot we can do about fieldmice,' I heard him saying, and winced, 'but let me know if there are any other problems. Au revoir!'

Pretentious berk, I comforted myself.

By the time I was washed and dressed, and possibly ready for a swim, Dan was back from the swimming-pool. 'It's getting really crowded now,' he said. 'Can't move for armbands and rubber rings. Fancy a walk down to the lake Soph? That's where it all happens, apparently, this year.'

Last year it had all happened round the football pitch for Dan. And me, really, but I'd only been thirteen then. I'd tagged along with a Dutch girl and we'd ridden bikes and swum and played crazy golf. I hadn't been aware of a 'scene'. This year I felt different. And I wouldn't have been seen dead playing football.

'OK,' I said. I suppose we had to start somewhere, though I'd actually quite felt like a swim.

'Go on, darling,' said Mum. 'You know you'll start enjoying yourself once you've made some chums.'

Chums. Good old Mum.

'That's my girl,' said Dad from where he was sitting in the car (go round any campsite and you'll find half the men sitting in their cars). 'Go and sort out the talent.'

Talent. Good old Dad.

Dan and I set off down the path that led through the woods, past the manoir and the tennis courts and down to the field by the lake. It was cool and green and the dust that we scuffed up as we walked shimmered in the shafts of sunlight that filtered through the leaves high above. After the trees the field seemed like a bright square with an even brighter strip of lake beyond it. There were a few kids out on the lake in pedaloes and some wrinklies fishing, but otherwise the place was almost deserted.

I raised an eyebrow at Dan. 'Happening, huh?'

'Well, it's humming with wildlife!' he said. It was true. The birds and the crickets made one hell of a racket. But no teenagers. We came to a heap of burned logs and ashes. 'Someone said something about bonfires,' he said.

'Looks like boy scout stuff to me,' I said. 'But you'd be more likely to have fires at night, wouldn't you?'

'Yeah. The people I heard it from were French, so I expect I got it wrong.'

'You were hanging around with *French* people?'

'We are in France.'

'Yes, but—'

'I want to improve my French.'

'Creep.'

'There is also this vision in an orange bikini, on a bike.'

'I haven't seen it. Gone off the waitress already then?'

'Bit old for me. Anyway, someone said she had one of the French couriers in tow.'

'You have been busy, listening.'

'Best way to learn.'

Lunch was bread and cheese and salad and wine. Simple fare, you might think. Yes, but not if you'd heard the parents raving over it. 'Wow – such cheap wine . . . *Gorg*eous cheese . . . *Pe*rfect bread – *noth*ing like it in England.' Tomatoes, 'Mwah!'

It was very hot after lunch. Dan disappeared on his bike and I was alone again. I really wanted a swim. I even saw a whole troop of teenagers – they did exist! – making their way to the pool, but I certainly wasn't going on my own.

'I'll sunbathe,' I told my sleepwalking parents – Mum had slipped her swimsuit straps down and Dad was snoring already. I slapped on the Factor 15 and stretched out on the sun lounger. I could at least start on the tan.

As I dozed off I heard the squealing brakes again and looked up expecting Dan. I was wrong. 'Hi Sophie!' said Jacy. 'It's OK, it's not you I'm after!' (Shame.) 'I'm checking out next door. You'll be getting neighbours this afternoon.' He disappeared into the empty tent on the other side of the hedge. I could hear him fossicking about in the fridge and banging the squeaky beds. Neighbours, eh? We already had Dutch neighbours on one side. Probably some family with a million screaming kids. That's what we usually get.

I was half asleep when they arrived. I heard Jacy's bike first, and then a clattery car. Lots of car doors banged. I rolled over onto my front so that I could peer at them. Their mum got out first, from the driving seat of an ancient clapped-out estate car. A pair of boys aged about eleven bundled out after her – twins I guessed – and rampaged around after Jacy. I was so taken up with

11

watching Jacy's lithe, tanned body in action that I was unprepared for more members of the family. Two older kids emerged, teenagers, a lumpy boy and a drippy looking girl. 'Come on Emma,' said the boy. 'Mam needs us.'

'OK,' said Emma. They had broad Geordie accents. There didn't appear to be a dad.

Isn't that just typical? The first time we ever get kids our age and they're a couple of unintelligible retards. I heard Jacy talking to their mum. 'The children's courier will be over in the morning. There's plenty of organised activities for the younger ones.'

'What about the teenagers?'

Jacy laughed. 'Ah,' he said, 'Don't worry about them Mrs Robson. You'll find that the less organisation they have, the better!' And he swung off on his bike.

I picked up a magazine and turned onto my back again. But I couldn't believe what I was hearing. 'You have a rest, like, Mam.' It was the girl. 'Mark and the boys are goin' a unload and I'm doin' the supper.' (Comedy Geordie accent here.) Their mum protested, but not much.

'Go on then, lads,' she said. 'Get to it!' So. Byker Grove comes to La Grange. I could have stayed home and watched the telly. I decided to make myself invisible before they tried to get friendly, and went inside the tent to catch up on my diary. At least I can say what I like there without anyone telling me I'm a snob/intolerant/narrow-minded/etc.

Dan came back – big smile on his face, big ice-cream in one hand. He threw his bike down. For once I felt quite glad to see him. But he spotted the newcomers and went over to talk to them instead.

'Hi,' he said. 'I'm Dan. Long journey?'

'You could say that,' said Mark. 'A day to come down

south from Newcastle. Overnight ferry and then driving through France today. We're shattered! And our mam's never driven in France before. Bit hairy on the round-abouts, eh Mam? I'm Mark by the way, an this is ma sister, Emma.'

'Hi,' said Emma. 'Is there anything for the likes of us to do on this site, then?'

'Come to the bar with us later,' said Dan. 'That seems to be where the evening starts. You should meet my sister. She's about the same age as you. See ya.'

He came on to our pitch. 'Weren't asleep were you?' he shouted noisily at the parents, waking them up. 'Where's Sophie then?' He saw me inside the tent.

'Dan!' I hissed. 'Why did you have to go and be all friendly to them? They're practically wearing shell suits for God's sake! We'll never get rid of them now!'

Dan looked at me uncomprehendingly. 'Why should we want to?' he said.

We were about to eat supper when Mark came over. 'Hey, Dan lad, care for a game of footie, like, after supper? The game starts at seven-thirty. Emma's playin'. Does your sister want-a come?' He looked at me. No. I did not want to play football.

'Sounds good to me,' said Dan. 'Coming to watch, Sophie?'

'I might, I said.

'We'll come and watch,' said Mum.

'Sounds like a fun evening to me,' I told her, but the sarcasm seemed to be lost on all of them.

I decided to roll up just as they finished so that I could at least go to the bar with Dan and maybe, just maybe, find some decent company. I couldn't stand the thought of being thrown together with drippy Emma. She'd set off wearing boys' football shorts and rubbish trainers. The Aire des Jeux (games area) was opposite the swimming-pool, behind the couriers' tents. It was a perfect evening and people sat watching on the bank as the players hurtled around the pitch. I found Mum and Dad. 'Dan's team are the ones without shirts,' said Dad. 'They had to put all the lasses in the other team – more's the pity!'

'Da-ad!'

'Young Emma's not a bad player, either.'

'No doubt,' I said, getting caught up in the game, in spite of myself. No one knew anyone else's name, so they simply shouted, 'Man on!' and 'Oy mate, over here!' or 'Ici! Ici!' It was a scramble, but clearly everyone was having a good time.

Emma scored a goal. The decider, what's more, so her and Mark's team – the shirts – were the winners. I even felt a slight twinge of jealousy as they came off. 'Big game next week,' said Dan to Dad. 'France v. England. The couriers are organising it.'

'Which team will our courier play for, then?' asked Emma. I knew she was daft.

I finally caught up with the 'scene' that night in the back room of the bar. And of course it had to include Emma and Mark. I discovered that Mark was sixteen and Emma fifteen. There were about twenty of us, mostly a bit older than me, though I know I look sixteen. Dan was right in there, but I didn't really know what to say to these weirdos. Things perked up briefly when Jacy poked his head round the corner. He seemed to be looking for someone. Me? (Well, you never know.) Surely not. But he caught my eye. 'Hi Sophie!' And then, 'Hi Emma.' What a letdown. Jacy was obviously one for the girls rather than the boys, but Emma, I realised with horror, had eyes only for Dan. When the others said they were going down to the lake I decided it was definitely time for bed.

Three

By the second morning La Grange starts to work its magic on you, however stressed-out you've been up until then. I poked my nose out of the tent. It was the misty prelude to a glorious day that's standard here, and it made me feel eleven years old again. I pulled on a pair of shorts and some trainers, grabbed a 100 franc note from where Dad had emptied his pockets the night before and set off on a round-the-camp route for the shop on Dan's bike. I pedalled like a kid, feeling the wind in my hair. Only a few people were about this early: one or two joggers and swimmers, dads with tiny children who'd been awake for hours. The bike ploughed satisfyingly through the sandy track, sending little stones skittering in our wake. The manoir loomed, gorgeous through the haze, silvery dew coating the hydrangeas and red hot pokers in the formal garden at the front. I scrunched to a halt by the shop and flung the bike down.

Huge crates of baguettes and croissants were piled up by the door – they smelt out of this world. I loaded up with Orangina and peaches and baguettes and waited in the queue to pay. Only when Jacy came in with wet hair and swimming shorts, with a towel round his shoulders and looking like an aftershave ad did I realise that I had bird's-nest hair, sleep in my eyes and a terrible T-shirt – and that I cared. I pretended I hadn't seen him and stuttered out my halting request for 'Quatre croissants au beurre, s'il vous plaît' in my best shopping French.

Jacy was picking out the ripest peaches with his back to me. He turned round as I waited for my change and called out across the crowded little shop in totally brilliant French, 'Bonjour Sophie! Tu achète le petit dejeuner, hein?' And then, 'What a good girl,' as I scuttled out into the morning sunshine, his sexy grin scorched, like the bright sun, onto my retinas.

I took great pleasure in waking up the others when I got back to the tent. The Dutch family were off to the showers in single file, perfect blonde mother with perfect tiny blonde daughters, father with comedy moustache carrying baby and leading little boy, all brown legs and good humour. Yuk. The Geordie twins were bent over their table, absorbed in twin-type activities, but there was no sign of Emma or Mark.

'Bog off, Sophie,' was all the gratitude I got from my brother. But Mum and Dad emerged tousled and smiling.

'Ooh! Peaches! Lovely, darling,' said Mum.

'I'll get some coffee on,' said Dad, and went to wash out the coffee pot.

'Did you hear Dan coming back last night?' asked Mum.

'No. Why?'

'Well, it was some terrible hour. I was quite worried. But I knew the two from next door were out too, so I wasn't as anxious as I might have been. I had a word with their mum. She said they were always up half the night in the holidays.'

'Probably doing community singing round the camp fire,' I said.

'Probably,' said Mum.

Dad came back. 'Thought we'd go to the supermarket this afternoon, Soph. Want to come?'

Now I'm a sucker for shopping, wherever it is. I like French supermarkets. And with the parents in a good mood there's often the opportunity to slip in the odd garment or bit of make-up, not to mention chocolate and other goodies. 'Yes, I'll come.'

'Good. Dan's keen. He wants to get a torch. We might check out the town, too. Eat out, even.'

'Don't get carried away, Dad.'

'I think I'll go and have a wash,' I said when I'd eaten what I wanted.

'I suppose we'll let you off the washing up, since you went to the shop,' said Mum.

'I should hope so too,' I said and gathered up everything I needed for a long session in the shower.

Dan still wasn't up when I got back. Next door the twins were batting a ball about and their mum was telling them to get off to the swimming-pool, otherwise they'd wake their big brother and sister. Oo-er. It *had* been a late night. Still, I didn't see why I should hang about all morning waiting for Dan. I went into the tent and banged on his canvas door. I unzipped and zipped the zip a few times. 'Wake up lazy bones!'

'Bog off Sophie!' There. He was at it again. I wasn't having this.

I put my head into his pit. 'Wakey, wakey! You know you want to get up and come swimming with me. I'll even let you have breakfast first. Mmmm, lovely croissants. Come on Dan!' I was getting impatient.

'Leave the poor lad alone!' That was Dad.

'Yes. Leave me alone.' I felt a major sulk coming on. This wasn't like Dan. I really didn't want to have to do things by myself.

'Come and buy some postcards with me,' said Mum. 'They sell them in the Acceuil – the reception bit by the bar.' She gave me a nudge. 'I just saw that dishy courier going in.' Oh great. I went with her, though, just for something to do. Fortunately Jacy wasn't there any more to see me doing things with-my-mum, but I had the sweaty palms and dry throat anyway. Mum laughed when we got in, and said in an embarrassing stage whisper, 'It's Dan I should have brought. Look who's on the desk.' I studied the postcards carefully for some minutes before turning around and seeing the waitress from the crêperie.

She smiled at Mum, ''Allo. 'Ow can I 'elp?'

'Well, well!' said Mum, laughing. 'How did you guess we were English?' and then struggled to speak in appalling French. I gave Mum the postcards I had chosen and legged it back to the tent.

– And ran slap-bang into Jacy again. Literally this time. 'Whoa there!' he said, gently levering me out of my head-butt. 'Throw yourself at me whenever you like, Sophie, but let me savour the anticipation next time!' I looked up at those laughing eyes and down again where he held my wrists. I was speechless. 'See ya!' he said, letting me go and tapping me lightly on the shoulder as he swung into the Acceuil. I was shell-shocked. Was that a come-on or what? The guy seemed to be everywhere. He was practically following me around. I walked on in a daze to our tent.

Dan sat at the table in his swimming trunks hunched over a croissant. He looked terrible.

'So it was a good night then?'

'Brilliant,' he said, between mouthfuls. 'Get us some Orangina, Soph.'

'Say please.'

'Please. I didn't get to bed till one or two!'

'A swim will do you good then. Oh come on, Dan. I haven't had a swim yet this holiday.'

'Who's fault is that? I'll come anyway, but just be gentle with me.'

I don't need to tell you that this is not typical Dan. But he's stubborn, our Dan, and I didn't want to upset him, not when I needed his company so badly.

'I suppose you won't let me go on my bike?'

'No. Walk with me. I don't want to go on my own.'

'OK, wimp.' We fetched towels and set off for the pool. The road across the top was heaving with parents and young children. Not a teen in sight, though given the early hour I shouldn't have been surprised. I assumed some of them would be bagging poolside places in the sun by now. I was right, but they weren't English teenagers. They were French. And one of them was the most stunning girl I have ever seen. She was wearing an orange bikini. It showed off her tan – so deep it was almost black – and voluptuous curves to perfection. She had beautifully cut brown hair that looked light and shiny compared to her skin, and green cat's eyes. So this was the vision in the orange bikini. I turned to Dan to say, yes, for once I see what you mean (and I hadn't even seen her on a bicycle), but Dan hadn't hung around for his embarrassment to show. He had dived into the pool.

The pool was otherwise occupied by kids having fun. And I mean kids. Screaming, splashing, divebombing, handstanding, snorkelling kids. Three years ago and I would have loved it. Now – it was hell. I couldn't even swim a length without bumping into several million of them. And I wasn't going to sunbathe. Not next to that French pussycat.

From the safety of the pool Dan waved at the French girls. 'Bonjour Francine! Bonjour Suzette!' he carolled.

'Hi Danny!' they replied, giving cute little waves.

'Suzette?' I asked him. 'As in crêpes?'

The French girls thought he was showing off for them. I might as well not have existed. 'Danny!' they called, leaping to their feet as all the dads' heads turned as one, and jumped into the water beside him, giggling. I watched. I'd agreed with Danny when he'd said they were out of his league, but they didn't seem to think he was out of theirs. There didn't seem to be much for me to do. I really didn't want to join in their ridiculous splashing games and watch my brother making an idiot of himself as he improved his French.

'I'm getting out Dan!' I called. 'Too crowded!'

'See you later then!' he said from the water. He clearly didn't need my company half as much as I needed his. 'A bientôt!'

I was starting to feel really sorry for myself as I slunk back to the tent. The day was heating up. I glanced towards the Suncampers office. It was quiet. Sonia was sitting outside, reading, glasses resting on her pointy little nose. Nor did my temper improve when I saw Mark and Emma chatting with Mum.

'Hi Sophie!' said Emma. 'Like your bikini!' Shame I couldn't say the same about hers.

'Hi Sophie!' said Mark. But he was all red and flustered and quickly went back to their tent, followed hotfoot by his sister. I fetched my book and the suntan lotion and dragged a sun lounger into the sun. There might not be anyone on this campsite worth talking to but at least I would go home brown. Now would have been a good time for Jacy to appear and ask if everything was OK. I kidded myself for a while that he might, arranging myself languorously on the lounger. He seemed to turn up everywhere else – why not here, and now? I'm sure I could convince him of my superior charms, given half a chance. Dream on, Sophie. Yeah, dream on!

Dan got back as we were about to start lunch. He'd caught the sun and looked, well – happy. 'You could have sunbathed by the pool, Soph,' he said. I didn't tell him why I hadn't. It's not like me to feel outclassed, even if she was French, and probably thick as two short planks. And probably a tart too.

'Bread, cheese and salad for firsts,' said Mum.

'And fruity little French tarts for afters,' said Dad. I couldn't have put it better myself.

The car was like an oven. Dan opened all the windows and the roof and waved at people as we drove off the site. I felt as though we were on different holidays. 'We're being followed by a vision in an orange bikini on a bicycle,' said Dad, looking rather too long in his rear-view mirror.

'That'll be Suzette,' I said.

'Ha! As in crêpes?' said Dad waggishly. I was about to put him down when I remembered I'd made the very same quip.

The supermarket was on the edge of the seaside town. Mum and Dad had the inevitable squabble about the importance or otherwise of parking in the shade. Then we went into air-conditioned shopping heaven. French supermarkets are huge and brilliant. They have CDs and stationery and clothes and shoes and crockery and bikes as well as food and cheap booze (cause for barely contained parental joy). We spent a happy couple of hours wandering up and down the aisles. I persuaded Mum to buy me a top and some flip-flops. Mum spent ages hovering over the Le Creuset. Dan lost himself first among the CDs and then the camping gear. Dad drifted from the cheeses to mustards to sausages in an ecstasy of bliss. We finally met up at the checkout. I'd managed to chuck in a few more things, like underwear and chocolate and felt at peace with France and the world. It was only when I thought for a moment that our goodlooking, tanned cashier was Jacy that I realised with a jolt that he hadn't popped into my mind for at least two hours. But

21

what does it mean when you think you see someone wherever you go?

We piled the shopping into the car and drove to the beach. It was a very French beach – civilised, with a small car park, lots of families with grannies and toddlers, people with big picnics in coolboxes, couples playing that silly game with little bats and a ball. Old men paddled, middle-aged women sunbathed without their tops on. Well, that was fairly gross, but in other ways it felt comfortable. If I had to be seen out with my family then I was glad it was a family beach.

It was quite good to be away from the campsite. I felt that social pressures were beginning to build up. I went for a paddle and thought about it all. It was annoying that Dan had made friends first, even though they were mostly people I wouldn't be seen dead with – like lumpy Mark and drippy Emma, and some of the others at the football match, or foreign like Francine and Suzette. Certainly none of the boys were anything to write home about, except of course, Jacy. There I was thinking about him again. Jacy makes the other boys look like kids. He's so fit. With a body like his he shouldn't be allowed to go around in swimming gear. And his voice, with that public school accent that makes him sound so confident. He *is* confident. He positively oozes confidence. And charm. But he's got a cute smile. And he seems to like me. I thought about the times I'd caught him eyeing me up. Not to mention 'throw yourself at me whenever you like'. I mean, I'm used to people fancying me, but it's rare for me to fancy them too. And he doesn't seem to have a girlfriend. It certainly isn't Coralie – though she is pretty gorgeous. Or Sonia? Unlikely. And that's the sum of British talent in his age group. Which leaves the field open for more youthful contenders – like me. I'm sure I could handle it. It's about time I had a proper mature boyfriend. Not an immature idiot like Ben Southwell.

At that moment a lightbulb seemed to switch on over my head. PROJECT! I did a little dance in the waves. Suddenly everything looked better. It was a challenge. *Jacy* was my challenge, my holiday romance! I was halfway there already, I was sure. I just had to impress him a bit. Show him how sophisticated I was. He probably thought I was sixteen anyway. A small aeroplane flew over the bay, trailing a banner. 'Bonnes vacances!' it said. Thank you, I thought. Don't mind if I do.

I jogged back, swooshing my feet through the shallows. I ran like a Baywatch babe. I ran like the wind . . . It's all right – help is on its way! The others had made a pitch under our green-and-yellow Suncampers umbrella, so they were easy to spot. Dad and Dan were delving into the coolbox. Mum was behind the umbrella chatting someone up. You can't take her anywhere! Still in Baywatch mode I dived under the umbrella and grabbed at Danny. 'Don't worry little boy! I'll rescue you!'

Dan swatted at me. 'Oy! Pamela! Lay off!' He shoved me into the sand and ran his cold can of coke up my back.

'Aaaagh!' I squealed and wriggled away, tipping the umbrella onto its side. There was Mum, looking down at us crossly.

'Kids!' she said, to Jacy – what was *he* doing here? (And what does it mean when you really *do* see someone wherever you go?) – 'Don't you love 'em?'

It was not easy to regain my composure, I can tell you. 'Hi Sophie,' said Jacy, with *that* look again. I sat up demurely. 'It's my day off – but can I get away from my job? My fault for coming to the nearest beach. I should know better than to get close to a green umbrella!' It was OK. He was laughing. 'I'm telling your Mum the best place to eat round here. And that's easy enough because I'll probably be going there myself later.' He turned to face the road into town. 'It's on the main road along the beach, just before you get to the apartment blocks. There's loads of restaurants but this one is called Hotel de Plage – I think. Blue-and-white awning, tables outside. Looks ordinary but the food is excellent, especially the *fruits de mer*.' He pronoucned it 'fwee de mare'. 'You haven't lived till you've eaten their *fruits de mer*.' He turned to go. 'Might see you later on then. I've got things to do in town now. Bye!' and he was off up the steps to the road.

'That was a spot of luck,' said Dad. 'It will be nice to go somewhere other than a pizzeria. Get a real taste of France. You kids are old enough for that now, of course. You wouldn't have let us a couple of years ago, it was pizzas or nothing in those days.'

I really enjoyed myself on that beach. I was buoyed up by 'Project Jacy', but for the time being he was conveniently in the town. With the prospect of a grown-up boyfriend it was as if I had permission to be a kid again. Danny was on good form and we mucked about in the waves for ages. We looked in rock pools and even – don't tell anyone – built a bit of a city in the sand. We attracted quite a gathering of *enfants* and Dan was directing them in his best French to find shells and seaweed or fetch buckets of water. Whenever we got too hot we just went in the sea again, slapped on more suntan lotion and carried on. The afternoon flew by. I couldn't believe it when Dad said it was after half-past seven and that he, for one, could eat a *cheval*.

My stomach gave a lurch. I should have been hungry too, but I actually felt slightly nervous at the thought of bumping into Jacy again. I had to remind myself that I probably had the upper hand here, as long as I stayed cool – and sophisticated. As far as I could see, being too young was my only problem.

The restaurant was in walking distance. We all felt slightly dazed from our afternoon in the sun. We decided to sit out on the street so we could watch the world going by (and I wanted to look out for Jacy).

We ordered drinks and the waiter brought us the menus. Dan put his down very quickly and said, 'I'll have the pizza.'

'Oh Dan,' said Mum. 'I thought you were going to be adventurous. I'm going to try the fish baked in cider. It's so fresh here.'

Dad was positively groaning with anticipation. 'Amazing. The French just *have* it, don't they? I'm completely spoilt for choice here. Some sort of fish is the obvious thing to go for. Ah! Crab soufflé! That sounds good. I'll go for that. And what about you Sophie?'

Well of course I wanted the pizza too, but as I read down the menu the words *fruits de mer* leapt out at me. *That's* what Jacy had been recommending. Fruits of the sea. Even my French could cope with that. Sounded OK. 'I'll have the *plateau de fruits de mer*, please Dad.'

'Ooh sweetheart,' said Mum. 'Are you sure?'

''Course I'm sure, Mum. I'm growing out of pizza, like you said. Have to try new things sometimes, don't you?'

'Well done, Sophie,' said Dad approvingly. 'Don't put her off, Sal. We should be encouraging her.' Mum smiled as the waiter came to take our order. Dan was smirking, but I don't know why. He'll still be eating pizzas when he goes out for business lunches.

'I wonder what's been going on at the campsite this afternoon,' said Dan as we waited for our food. 'I told them all I'd go down the pool this afternoon.'

'All of them, eh, Dan? I don't know how any of them

will survive without your scintillating company, let alone the lovely Emma.'

'Don't knock Emma,' said Dan shortly.

'Sorr-*y*. Didn't know you cared.'

'They're people, Emma and Mark.'

'Oh, sorry. I hadn't realised.'

We didn't get any further. 'Look, you two,' said Mum. 'Our food's coming.'

Dan was served his pizza with a flourish. A second waiter came along with Mum's fish and Dad's crab soufflé. 'Don't mind me,' I said. 'Go ahead and start.' Secretly I was pleased that mine hadn't come. There was still a chance that Jacy might turn up and see me eating sophisticated *fruits de mer*. I kept thinking I could see him coming our way, but then there were quite a few dark-haired guys with tanned skin and white T-shirts around.

Dan was half-way through his pizza when our waiter appeared carrying an enormous plate. Could this be what I had ordered? He put it down in front of me with a smile. 'Bon appetit, Ma'mselle.'

Oh . . . my . . . God.

This plate had eyes and feelers. It had disgusting globby things and jellyish things. It had shells and legs.

And there was Jacy sitting down a few tables away, with Sonia.

Jacy saw us and waved. Then he turned back to Sonia. She said something to him and he looked up again. Looked straight at me. He was trying to say something without shouting across the other tables. I tried to make out what it was he was saying. Then I realised. It was 'Bon appetit!'

So that was it. I was going to have to eat the things. All around us other people were tackling hideous platefuls. I watched them carefully. I copied them. Gloop went an oyster. I shuddered as it went down. Eughh. Glop went a mussel. It tasted of seawater. Snap, crack, scoop, went the half lobster – that wasn't so bad actually. I tore off lots of bread, ate it and ploughed on. Dan finished his pizza and looked on admiringly, his mouth open. 'Well done, Sophie!' said Dad. 'Tackled like a native!'

'Are you sure you can manage all that, darling?' Mum was looking anxious. She'd nearly finished her fish. 'What a dark horse you are. I had no idea you liked seafood.' I didn't answer. I was concentrating too hard on getting the revolting stuff out of its shells and down my throat. I kept refilling my glass with water and washing it down. Every now and then I caught a glimpse of Jacy over the way. His head bobbed around as he talked to Sonia. I saw them ordering but no food seemed to appear.

I was nearly there. I had to be. Mum, Dad and Dan had finished ages ago. Dad and Dan were deep in discussion about the exchange rate and Mum was happily getting squiffy on white wine. Maybe I didn't have to finish it. Maybe it would be cooler to leave a bit – as if it was no big deal. I decided to let myself off the last few and sat back with a sigh. I looked up to see Sonia's and Jacy's meals arriving. They were having pizza.

I started to feel queasy on the way back in the car. The sick feeling didn't go away. It got worse. 'Dad! Stop the car! I'm going to be sick!'

Mum looked over at me. 'Oh my goodness, Giles! She's gone green!' Dad pulled over as soon as he could. I only just got out in time. I threw up. Copiously.

Mum put me to bed as soon as we got back to the campsite. I felt terrible. Hot and achey as well as queasy. My head was pounding and my legs felt leaden. I felt shivery as well as burning. Mum's a good nurse, she didn't panic. She found me a bottle of cold mineral water and wiped my forehead with a flannel. Dad flapped about. 'Do you think she needs a doctor? Do you think we should ask the couriers? Do you think it was all that seafood. Perhaps it's food poisoning!'

'She'll be fine. I don't think it's just the meal. I think she had too much sun. Anyway, we know that two of the couriers aren't even here.' I didn't really want Jacy to know I had thrown up my sophisticated meal but I was past caring. I wanted everyone to go away and leave me to die in peace. But not even my body would allow me to do that. I was up and down most of the night staggering to the toilet block. How I wished we were in a caravilla with its own loo. How I wished that somehow the divine Jacy would come and make me better.

Four

I slept quite late in the morning. I could tell when I woke up that it was very bright outside, and the campsite noises were mostly of cars starting up as people left for the beach. I turned away from the light and let the day come at me gently. I no longer felt sick. My skin felt hot and dry and I ached a bit, but apart from that I felt more or less like a human being.

There's not much you can do in a tent without being heard. My bed obviously creaked enough to let Mum know that I was awake. The zip of my compartment opened and her head appeared. 'How are you feeling this morning, sweetheart?'

'Bit better.'

'Would you like me to bring you a drink?'

'It's OK Mum. I can get up. I need to go to the loo anyhow.' I started to get out of bed. It was harder than I thought. My burnt bits felt really stiff. Down came the zip.

'Let me help you.' I staggered into the open. Boy, was that sun bright. 'Sunglasses, that's what you need.' Mum plucked hers off her nose and put them on mine. The relief was instant. Her bathrobe was on the chair and she wrapped it over my T-shirt and knickers and walked me to the toilet block. I looked at the ground. Mostly I felt too lousy to care, but I wasn't totally keen on meeting people looking like this. I should add that Mum's bathrobe is extremely ancient pink towelling and hideous and that her sunglasses look like something Edna Everage would wear.

When we got back she hustled me into the living room bit of the tent and pulled the gingham curtains across the plastic windows, but not before I saw Emma, Mark, the twins, a twin-aged friend and a large teenage girl all lined up looking at me. And not before my eagle eye spotted the designer label on the large girl's jeans. I'd have to be more than ill for a Moschino label to escape my notice. Danny, as my brother, felt permitted to say, 'Now there's a sight for sore eyes,' much to everyone's amusement.

'Yeah, hilarious,' I grumbled as Mum sat me down in front of a sliced peach and a glass of mineral water. I could *hear* them laughing.

Dan came in. 'Just going over to Becky's, Mum.'

'Will you be back for lunch?'

'Probably.'

'Dan!' I called back. 'Is Becky the one in the Moschino jeans?'

'I dunno,' said Dan. 'She's the one out there if that's what you mean. See ya!'

Fancy not noticing jeans as classy as that. Even if she was quite fat. Good taste, though. She might be worth getting to know. I turned my attention to my peach – as far as Mum would let me. '*Every*one's been asking after you,' she said. 'Mark was very concerned – and their mum. And that nice Dutch family next door. And the couriers, they all asked after you. Even Jesse.'

Jesse? 'Jacy, Mum, as in Jaycee.' Hmm. How did Jacy know? Was I pleased at his concern? Anyway, it was sunstroke, Mum said so, nothing to do with eating seafood.

'I think you'd better stay under cover today.' Mum went on. 'We can bring one of the sunbeds in for you to lie on.'

'But Mum,' I protested. 'I'll die of boredom!'

'No you won't. You've got your Walkman and your novels. You could write some postcards.'

'That will be scintillating.'

'We want you to get better. Perhaps Daniel will bring some of his friends to visit you.'

'That will *really* make me feel better.' Though of course, if *Jacy* came to visit me I might start to revive a little . . . I got dressed, just in case I did have visitors. Mum fussed about to make me comfortable. Then she got to the point of her fussing. 'Dad really wants to go to the market in La Roche this morning. I'll stay behind and look after you if you want, but if you're really feeling much better, we'd only be an hour or so—'

'Go to market, Mum. I'll be fine,' – especially without you fussing over me.

'Emma and Mark's mum has offered to pop in from time to time, see if you need anything . . .'

'Mum – go!'

I was on my own. I tried reading. It made my eyes tired. I lay down and listened to my Walkman for a bit. I thought about postcards. I could send one to Hannah – not that there was much to say. I don't think she'd be very interested in hearing about Jacy, and not a lot else has happened to me. I delved around in my bag. Good, it was there – my DIARY. That would pass a bit of time. It's one of those big hardbacked exercise books. Some days I write masses in it. And I decorate the pages, do fancy lettering, stick stuff in. I pulled it out and turned through it. There was the page I'd scribbled recently but the last thing I'd stuck in before that were some photos of the sleepover. There was Hannah without her glasses and trying make-up on. It was quite an improvement. Charlotte stuffing her face – as usual. Maddy, suffering from red-eye in this picture. And there was one we'd set up of us all dancing about. I looked quite good in that one, though I say it myself. I'd shoved in the note from Ben Southwell. Not sure why. Aagh. *Fresh* page, I think. Perhaps I'll write about Jacy. I wrote in pencil. Then I could rub it out if it got too embarrassing.

Let me describe Jacy, the only good thing about this terrible holiday. He's quite tall and incredibly fit with short dark hair and a terrific tan. He's got hairy legs and arms but not a hairy chest. His skin's a beautiful colour. He's got quite a good 6-pack and he looks amazing. The best thing about him is his eyes, though all his face is OK – good cheekbones. His eyes are hazel and shiny sometimes, and melty other times with very black eyelashes. He has this way of looking at you that's so sexy. I've heard Mum describing someone as having 'bedroom eyes', and I think that probably describes him perfectly. Definitely a 'man', though I think he's probably only about 18 or 19.

What else? Oh yes. Probably the sexiest thing of all (so far!) is his voice. Kind of deep and soft with this slightly public-school accent – the sort Mum likes and I usually don't like (intolerant as I am) – but it makes him seem very self-assured (is that the right word? – sure of himself anyway). Could almost be smarmy, but somehow with him it isn't. And he seems to have quite a good sense of humour.

Someone was coming. My God – it was Jacy. I could hear him talking to the Dutch kids. They were saying 'Jacy! Jacy! You want to play football?' and he was saying, 'Later, later!' and laughing. There was someone with him.

Damn! It was drippy Mark.

I heard Jacy say goodbye and walk off. But Mark – aagh, *Mark* – came onto our pitch. 'Er – Sophie?' He said it quite quietly, in case I was asleep I suppose, but it was ridiculous considering how loudly the Dutch kids had been yelling. 'Er – Sophie? Me mam said as how I were to see how you were doin'?' He came round the corner to where he could see me. Should I pretend to be asleep or not? Too late. 'Oh. There you are. Do you want anythin', Sophie? I've brought a bottle of nice cold water.' He came in to the tent – *not* that I invited him. And he sat down. At the table. I hastily shut my diary, but not before he said, 'Ma sister keeps a diary an' all.'

There wasn't an answer to that, and he'd dried up all of a sudden. Nothing was said for a few moments and then, 'Do you want anythin', Sophie? I've brought a bottle of nice cold water.' Change the record, Mark. 'I'm goin' a get an ice-cream, right. D'ya want one?' Actually, an ice-cream sounded fab at that moment. And if Mark was prepared to get one I wasn't going to refuse.

'OK.'

'D'ya want an ice-cream?'

'Yes, that's what I said.' We had a bit of a language problem here.

He looked stunned. Then blushed. Then smiled a slow grin. Uh-oh! 'You really want me a get you an ice-cream?'

'YES!' . . . Perhaps he was waiting for me to say please.

'Yes please, Mark. A vanilla one would be champion.' Did I really say *champion*? Well, you have to speak the lingo to get results.

'Right. Like, right.' And he tottered off. What had happened to the guy? I mean, I know he's not up to much, but he seemed to have lost his marbles completely.

I picked up my diary and wrote.

Now let me describe Mark. Mark is fair and pasty and spotty. He is large and gawky. His skin is kind of pink and pudgy. His fingers are like sausages. Someone should buy him a shaving kit. His armpits niff. And I expect his trainers do too. His eyes are blue. On a scale of one to ten for sex appeal he rates minus five. What else can I say? Oh yes. Personality. What person-ality? Mark suffers from complete lack of personality, as does his sister Emma. Also lack of taste, humour, etc.

He was coming back – running, even. He shot into the tent before I had time to close my diary, but it wasn't him, it was two of them, one on each side of me, one accidentally knocking my diary onto the ground, the other thrusting an ice-cream at me. 'Ooh, ma sister writes a diary, an' all,' said one twin.

'Oy,' I bellowed, twisting over to shut the diary.

'Mark would have brought ya the ice-cream,' said one.

'But he got detained, like,' said the other.

'By Becky!' said the first one.

'*Big* Becky,' said the second – and they both cracked up and ran off to their tent, leaving me with a dripping ice-cream and feeling slightly confused. That's twins for you.

I decided to put the diary under the table before anyone else saw it. But visiting hours weren't over yet. It was Mark, again. 'Did ya like ya ice-cream, like?'

'Yeah, thanks,' I said not terribly graciously. I wanted him to go away.

'Did ya like ya ice-cream, like?' he asked again with an asinine grin. Oh please God, no. Not this repetition stuff again.

I was about to say, 'Yeah, cheers, thanks a lot,' when he said something different.

'Becky's comin' by. She wants a meet ya.'

Becky filled the doorway of the tent. As a silhouette she was large. Not just tall but loads of puppy fat and big hair. 'Hi!' she said. She had a surprisingly light voice. Quite posh. 'I just *had* to meet the girl who was Dan's sister, not to mention Mark's next-door-neighbour!' She sat down at the table with me. 'You coming or going, Mark? Think you'd better keep an eye on those kids, don't you?'

'Ah!' said Mark and went to their tent. I could hear him repeating the 'Ah!' as he went.

'Real sweetheart, Mark. You seem to render him speechless, though. I've known him for two days now and I've never seen him so lost for words! You've got fairer hair than your brother, haven't you? Bet it's natural. Mine isn't.'

'It gets bleached in the sun,' I said.

'Why haven't I seen you before? Don't you get on with your brother, or something? You're really lucky having Emma and Mark next door. It's all little kids round us. Like my little brother. He's a complete pain, though it's much better now he's discovered Tweedledum and Tweedledee over there. I'd much rather have an older brother. Especially one like Dan. He's cool.'

'Danny? Cool?' It was beyond belief that this girl in her Moschino jeans and her DKNY top (I now noticed) could think that Danny was cool.

'Yeah. And he said straightaway that he thought you and I would be into the same things!'

34

He was more observant than I gave him credit for. 'Where's your tent?'

'Miles away. Out on the prairie. It's a caravilla, actually. Suncampers though, same as you. Hey, have you got the same sexy courier as we have, Jacy?'

I kicked my diary right under the table. 'I think so,' I said cautiously.

'He's gorgeous, don't you think? You're probably used to gorgeous guys though. I can't believe you're only fourteen. I'm nearly sixteen, though I don't look it, do I? Probably because I go to a girls' school. They try to stop us growing up by putting us in a hideous uniform. We don't really get to meet boys. My parents say I can go clubbing when I'm sixteen, but my dad's ever so protective. He thinks we're really safe here – all good clean fun sort of thing.'

'I know. And he's probably right. Pity, isn't it!'

'Do you know, he even went up to the girl on the bar, pointed me out and said – "That one is still fifteen. If I find out she's been served alcohol, I'll know who to blame." Luckily, she's French and didn't know what he was on about!'

Mum and Dad's car drew up at that point, followed by the tell-tale squeal of brakes that heralded Dan's arrival. Becky looked at her Storm watch and said, 'I'd better drag my little bro back home for lunch. Pity it's so far. I'm even contemplating hiring a bike. Wish I had my horse!'

'Hi Becky!' said Dan, as if he'd known her all her life. 'Pool this afternoon?'

'Of course!' she replied. 'Pool in the afternoon. Bar in the evening. Bonfire down at the lake tonight. See you later!'

'Thought you two would get on,' Danny said to me, breaking off half a French loaf from the shopping and gnawing at it. 'Don't suppose you'll be coming swimming will you?'

I started to say Possibly, but Mum interrupted. 'Certainly not. I might let you out again in the cool of the evening, but you're not going out in the full sun today.' She and Dad put lunch on the table inside the tent and we all sat down to it. 'It's unbelievably hot out there right now, isn't it Dan? In fact you'd better take care down at the pool this afternoon. Apparently Mark got a bit burnt yesterday.' Dan didn't answer. I felt unreasonably irritable at him. I realised how great it would be to have a girl my own age to natter to. I could have kicked myself at completely missing the simplicity of the 'scene' that Becky described. I'd been in the wrong place every time. Unlike Dan.

'I don't think I want to be there anyway,' I said nastily. 'It's bad enough being caught in the cutesy crossfire from French bimbos, but the vision of Mark with a sunburnt torso might just make me feel ill all over again.'

'Shh!' said Dan. 'You seem to forget these walls are canvas. They can hear every word we say, you know.'

'Ah! But can they understand it?'

Dan turned on me. He spoke in a hoarse whisper. 'I do not understand you, Sophie Morris. You are just *such* a snob. They (he pointed next door) are perfectly OK people, really friendly, and all you can do is rubbish them because *you* have a problem understanding their cool accent. As for (and he mouthed "Mark") – well, he's actually taken in by the Sophie Morris mystique, says he's never met a girl quite like you before. I think he should count himself lucky. He's probably never met anyone who's been so unpleasant to him.'

I couldn't for the life of me see why Dan was so worked up. 'But he's such a cretin, Dan. He kept coming in here and bothering me this morning, with water and ice-cream and stuff.'

'Oh dear,' said Mum. 'I thought their mother was going to pop in. I didn't mean her to ask the children.'

Dan spoke before I could add anything. 'Mark wanted to, Mum. He's OK. He felt really sorry for Sophie because he'd got sunburned too and knew how it felt. He spent ages deciding what to take her. We were all in the bar before lunch. It was Jacy who suggested the mineral water from the fridge. I expect that makes it OK now, does it Sophie?'

Well, it certainly made it a bit better. Fancy Jacy thinking about what would be best for me.

'Well, Sophie, does it?' Dan wanted an answer. I couldn't think of one. If he couldn't see that Jacy's attentions were more welcome to me than Mark's, then he needed his head examining.

I tried to think of something smart to say. 'Just because you fancy Mark's sister doesn't mean I have to fancy Mark.' It wasn't smart, because Dan's sensitive about that sort of thing and it just made him angry.

'You're a pain in the bum, Sophie. I've a good mind to tell – (and he nodded next door again) what an ungrateful old moo you are. Might just tell Jacy as well.'

'Children, children!' said Dad. 'If you can't say any-thing nice then don't say anything at all.'

'Sit in the shade this afternoon, Sophie. Then maybe you can join the others in the evening. I don't want you to miss out on any of the fun.' Good old Mum. There was me having a huge row with Dan that was about to ruin the whole awful holiday and she hadn't caught on at all. But she did make Dan do the washing up.

Dan still wasn't speaking to me when he set off to the pool. There were shady spots outside the tent now, so I buried my diary deep in my bag, found a novel and my

Walkman and dragged a sunbed as far from the hedge we shared with next-door as possible. I was a tiny bit worried that they might have overheard us at lunchtime, but I can't say I really cared. Mum and Dad were having a snooze after their morning's exertions. Sleep seems to come very easily on these occasions. It wasn't long before I dropped off too.

'Hi Sophie!' It was Becky. She and Emma had arrived on bicycles. They were both in bikinis. Quite a contrast. Emma is small and neat with (I have to admit) a good figure. Becky is the opposite. Her copious flesh was not a pretty sight, but the bikini was something to die for. It must have cost at least £80. 'See you later, Emma!' Becky called after her. 'Have a good tennis lesson!' She leant her bike against a tree and came over. 'You awake, Sophie? Do you want to come down to the lake?'

'I have to stay in the shade,' I said.

'Plenty of shade down there. I got too hot by the pool, and I don't like to keep jumping in the water because this bikini goes transparent. Your mum would let you, wouldn't she?'

'That's all right. I just won't ask. I'll come. I'm going stir-crazy anyway, and I feel OK now.'

'I'll leave my bike here then. We can spy on Emma's tennis lesson on the way down.'

I pulled on a blouse and some shorts. As a concession to Mum I wore a baseball cap as well. I even scribbled a note which I weighted down with a stone. 'Gone to sit in shade somewhere else with Becky.' We set off through the woods, the same way I'd been with Dan on our first day. Not many people were around. A few people on bicycles. A group of kids on ponies. Far off we caught glimpses of Coralie and Sonia with a line of singing junior Sun-campers. We came to the gap in the hedge at the side of the manoir where there were three tennis courts. People were having coaching – they didn't seem to mind the heat of the day.

'That's what Emma's doing next,' said Becky. 'By the way, why don't you two like each other?'

'What?' I was taken aback. OK, I didn't like Emma, but only Dan knew that. Didn't he?

'She says you don't like her, but she doesn't really mind. She just thinks you're a bit snobby about northerners.' Becky said all this in her even-toned, light voice. I looked at her but it was obvious she wasn't being spiteful, just passing on information.

'I suppose I don't really know her,' I conceded.

'Yeah, that's what I said,' said Becky. 'After all, all the rest of us know each other pretty well now, but you've been ill haven't you?'

I wanted to say that the rest of them couldn't really know each other that well – none of them had been here more than a few days – and that I'd only genuinely been out of action since last night, but I liked Becky and, I realised, I needed her. Heaven knows what 'they' had all been saying about me when I wasn't there. I wasn't even sure that I could rely on Danny to take my side. It wasn't looking good. And it wasn't what I was used to. Best to change the subject.

'Who does the tennis coaching?'

'Oh, I don't know their names, but they are these fabulous French guys. French guys are *so* sexy, don't you think?'

Well, I couldn't really agree with her there. 'Have you ever done any riding here?'

'Oh yes.' Horses were definitely still very much on the agenda for Becky. 'I'm down for one on Friday. Hey, why don't you come too? Emma can't afford riding as well as tennis. Oh go on, it would be brilliant.'

I didn't really want to be a substitute for Emma, but I

did quite fancy a ride. Get away from my folks, from the campsite. 'I'll ask,' I said.

We wandered on down the path to the open field in front of the lake. Even with shades and a hat the bright square of light exploded into our faces as we emerged from the wood. 'Wow. It's a bit bright,' said Becky. 'Let's go along the edge of the wood in that direction. There's a stream that runs into the lake and we could sit on the bridge.' I followed her.

We sat on the bridge dangling our feet in the water. It was blissful. 'Where are you from, Becky?' I assumed she was a home counties sort of person, what with a horse and everything, but you never know, do you?

'Just outside Chester.'

Oh God, where is Chester? I thought I wouldn't ask, given what people thought about me already. It might be in the north.

'Hollyoaks has really put us on the map!' she added.

I watch Hollyoaks, but I still don't know where Chester is.

'It's great for shopping,' she said. 'But of course we're not far from Liverpool and Manchester.'

Great. Clues. So it *is* in the north.

'What about you? You and Dan both speak like southerners.'

'London,' I said. I'd never considered myself as a 'southerner' before. 'But quite a long way out.'

'Wow!' She said it as if I came from Mars. 'Don't you just spend all your time wanting to buy things?'

The sun had moved around. The lake glittered invitingly. 'Shall we see if we can grab a pedalo?' I asked. 'It doesn't look so lethal out there any more.' We jumped down from the footbridge and made our way over to the little jetty where one of the pedaloes was beached. They were there for anyone to use.

'I rode one of these round with Mark for ages last night,' said Becky as we climbed in. 'We were trying to ram Danny and Suzette, but they were too fast for us.'

'Do you mean my brother shared a pedalo with the orange bikini girl?' I asked, pedalling furiously.

'Suzette, yes! She won't leave him alone!' said Becky laughing. 'Emma's dead jealous. She thinks Dan's wonderful. Now I've nothing against blond blokes, but on the whole I think I go more for the lean, mean mediterranean look. Not that anyone answering that description would look twice at me!' she said comfortably. And, silently, I had to agree with her. 'You, on the other hand, are totally drop-dead gorgeous. I bet you could find a fab French guy.'

'Not all that keen on the French,' I said.

'Have you got a boyfriend then?' she asked.

I didn't want to give much away. 'Sort of,' I said vaguely. We let our boat drift about.

Becky looked over to me. Her mind was obviously still on romance. 'Who do you fancy here then?'

'Oh, no one really. They all seem a bit young.'

'Well, what about the couriers? You must have noticed Jacy, our courier. I'm sure he *is* yours too. Now he would make the perfect boyfriend for you.'

'Do you think so?' I said, rather too quickly.

'Oh yes! Why didn't I think of it before! You kind of go together. You're all slim, blonde and beautiful and he's bronzed, dark and handsome – the perfect couple!' Becky was away. I didn't need to say anything. 'Now, how can we get you together? You must come to the bar more. He's always hanging around the bar. Ooh! Isn't this fun? I simply love matchmaking!' We pedalled the boat back to the jetty.

As we walked back to our tent my head was still swirling with angry thoughts about Danny. I wanted to hurl insults at him and our stupid neighbours. But then I remembered that they all went to the bar in the evenings and that the bar was also where Jacy hung out and that it was where I wanted to be. I was going to have to make my peace with Dan, but that didn't mean I had to pretend to like big Mark and drippy Emma. I could manage without them.

Five

The afternoon had got hotter and hotter and more humid. Even now, with supper nearly over, it seemed unnaturally warm, like a bath, and airless. I'd tried to apologise to Dan without grovelling and blamed the fact that I'd been ill. He was still fairly cool, but I felt that we were no longer at war. Emma passed by with their washing up. She put her head round the corner. 'Hi Dan! coming up to the bar later?'

'I'll be there!' he said.

'Can I come up with you?' I asked tentatively.

'Suppose so,' he said. 'As long as you're not snotty with my friends.'

'I'm not snotty with Becky.'

'I didn't mean her.'

'And Becky's not snotty with anyone.'

'That's true. But you know what I mean.'

I thought it would be politic to grovel just a little at this point. 'Yes Dan. I'll try to be friendly. But—'

'But nothing.'

'Yessir!'

'You seem much better, Sophie,' said Mum. 'Do you think you are?' I did. I felt recovered, just a bit stiff. My afternoon at the lake with Becky had cured me. Things were looking up.

The bar had a back room that was packed with teenagers. We bought our drinks from the French waitress and carried them through. Becky had saved a place for me. She had changed into a gorgeous Kookai blouse with her Moschino jeans. She was wearing make-up too, though I thought she could do with some sorting out in that department. I'd put on a short white dress. I know it suited me and it showed off my legs, since my tan was now coming along nicely. Emma was sitting next to Becky. She was making cow eyes at Dan again. Yuk. He plonked himself next to her, what's more. Her evening gear consisted of cyling shorts and a belly top. Mark wasn't with her, but there were various other people there who I had seen waving to Dan. It was definitely a British group. Francine and Suzette were chatting with the girl at the bar and the Dutch seemed to have their own thing going outside. And to think our parents all bring us here to mix with European youth!

I'd spotted Sonia and Coralie as we came in. They were sipping bright blue drinks that looked lethal. No Jacy though. 'I wonder where Jacy is,' whispered Becky, louder than I liked. 'He's not propping up the bar like he usually is.'

Luckily no one heard her, and I was able to pretend I hadn't either because some raucous lads were asking Dan to be introduced to his sister 'and her legs'. John and Steve were Liverpudlians. I couldn't understand a word they said, but I could tell they were funny. And what seemed to fuel their jokes more than anything was the way Becky and I spoke! They found everything we said hilarious, even simple words like 'bar' and 'chair' (try saying them with a Liverpool accent) creased them up. I could see we were in for a jolly evening.

This was more like it – Becky and me being chatted up by two admiring blokes. Well, I felt pretty confident that they admired me, anyway. I felt happier than I had done all holiday. They kept buying us drinks, too. After last night's little episode I thought I'd better stick to soft drinks, and Becky, despite her brave words, was actually still afraid of her Dad catching her boozing, so there was lots of ice and lemon clinking about. The lads were downing *demis* and getting noisier as the night wore on.

Outside, the air was hot and soupy. Inside it was hot and plain sticky. There was talk of going down to the lake, but it felt as though it was going to thunder any minute. I felt a bit dodgy and went for some fresh air – but there wasn't any. I stood at the open door of the bar. The front of the bar was full of adults. My parents were there with the Dutch neighbours and Mark and Emma's mum. Little children were threading their way between the tables. There was a general air of excitement. It really felt as if the sky was about to break open. And then, as I was standing by the door, it did. There was a tremendous flash of lightning that tore the sky in two, followed by great echoing rolls of thunder. People outside squealed and headed for the bar as great fat drops of rain started to fall. I was joined by the French barmaid. She peered anxiously through the rain, but pulled back as a large figure in long shorts and wet plimsolls splattered over the tarmac and ducked into the doorway, shaking drips everywhere like a dog.

It was Mark. Drippy Mark, even! 'It's OK, Hélène,' he said to the barmaid. 'Your feller's on his way. The lightning missed him too. An' I need a drink!' Seeing her incomprehension he made drinking motions with his hand and shooed her back towards the bar. She tittered and gave him her lovely smile. I have to admit, it was a different Mark. Then he turned and nearly fell over me. I saw the change come over his face. 'Oh. Sophie,' he stuttered. 'Oh. Sophie. I didn't see you there. Can I buy you a drink?'

'No thanks,' I said, and squeezed my way through to the back room again. The French girls had materialised and were sitting with Dan. Orange bikini, now in an orange blouse, was being particularly friendly. Emma was looking bootfaced and called to Mark that she'd help him with the drinks.

'Yes please!' shouted Becky. 'Coke for me! With ice and lemon.'

Mark put his head round. 'Anyone else? Dan? Sophie – are you sure you don't want anything?'

'Quite sure, thanks,' I said. 'I told you already.' There was a short silence. Becky looked over at me as I sat down. 'I wish he'd leave me alone,' I said to her.

'Lad was only offering to buy you a drink,' said one of the Scousers, somewhat disapprovingly.

'Yes, well. You wouldn't understand,' I told him.

He put his hands up to show he was backing off. 'Good-looking girl like you. I expect blokes are always trying to chat you up.'

'It can get tiresome,' I said.

'Lucky old you,' said Becky. 'I wouldn't complain!'

I sat back. I could hear the thunder receding as the rain grew steadier, beating on the roof and slanting across the windows. I wondered where Jacy was. I flicked my hair back and stretched out my legs. Mark and Emma came in with the drinks and started handing them round. Then, would you believe it, Mark came and sat next to me! He was all squelchy from the rain and disgusting. Can't that guy take a hint? And what did he say? He said, 'Er, Sophie, are you sure you don't want a drink?'

'No, Mark. I do not want a drink.' I couldn't stand this

klutz any longer. I got up, pushed past him and went to the loo.

When I came out I wasn't sure what to do. I hoped Dan hadn't heard me snapping at Mark. I knew Emma had, but then she had already decided I was a snob. I suddenly felt a bit unsure of Becky and the Liverpool lads. Was I really behaving badly? Did I care what they thought of me? I didn't mean to be unkind, but they obviously, Becky in particular, had no idea what it was like to be followed about. It happens to me all the time. Lovesick blokes. It's not as if they're any fun. Don't they realise how boring they are? If only Jacy would come in.

I looked towards the open doorway. The dark square was lit up for a moment by blue lightning, and, as if in answer to my prayer, there was Jacy. And what a vision he was! His wet T-shirt was plastered to his pecs and his hair was slick with rain. Water ran down his face as he smiled towards me at the bar. A gorgeous, warm, melting smile.

'Hi Jacy!' I called. 'Do you want a drink?'

'I'll get it, thanks,' he said. 'I get an extra special discount, don't I, Hélène?' He winked at the French barmaid. 'I'll join you in the back bar in a minute.'

So. My decision was made for me. I made my way through the crush towards Becky. Mark was still sitting there, but he leapt to his feet clumsily as I approached. 'You'll be wantin' a sit down. Here.' I didn't wait to be asked twice this time.

'We've decided to give the lake a miss tonight,' said Becky.

'Hardly the weather for a bonfire!' added John. I noticed he and Becky were sitting so close that Becky was practically on his lap.

Jacy appeared. I could see his wet seal-head above a group of girls. So did Becky. She nudged me hard, nearly spilling Coke over my white dress as she shot her other hand in the air like an eager schoolgirl. 'Over here Jacy!' she called, and squeezed up even closer to John to make more room for me and of course Jacy. He was carrying one of those virulent blue drinks. My God, he really was going to sit with us, with me to be precise. He perched himself on the end of the bench, right next to me. He was still damp from the rain and steaming gently. Wow! So was I. He leant in to me and Becky. 'How are you doing, girls? No bonfire tonight, then?' (There's one right here, did you but know it, I felt like saying.) He took a sip of his drink. 'That's better.' He sat back. 'It's been a busy night. Campers don't like rain. It'll be sunny again tomorrow though. It always is after a thunderstorm. And the girls have gone back to take over for a bit, so I'm sort of off-duty.' He drank the blue stuff thirstily.

I was intrigued. 'What's that drink called? It looks pretty powerful!'

'Oh, haven't you ever tried it? It's called Bleu Tropique. Here, have a swig – but go easy!' He wiped the rim of his glass rather engagingly and passed it over to me. I sniffed it cautiously. It smelt strong, like some of the cocktails Hannah and I once experimented with.

'Hey! That's nice!' It was a lot nicer than any of the other ice and lemon drinks I'd had that night.

'Would you like one? I'll get you one if you like.'

'I'd love one,' I said boldly, though he'd already slipped off to the bar, leaving me feeling surprisingly bereft without his damp warmth against me. There was movement amongst the others in the back bar and I prayed that Mark wouldn't take the place left by Jacy. I shifted over slightly to fill it myself and turned to Becky and John and Steve so that I shouldn't look as if I was on my own.

'You're doing OK there!' said Becky excitedly. 'Where's he gone?'

'To buy me a drink,' I said smugly.

'Must have more money than us then,' said Steve. 'I've run out now.'

'Still,' said John, nudging Steve, 'He does get that *special* discount at the bar . . .'

'Don't know what you're talking about,' said Steve, smiling broadly at Becky and me. 'I'm going back for my beauty sleep now. See you guys. Don't get too drunk Sophie!' And he edged out from the table, sitting on each of us as we went, accompanied by lots of squealing from Becky, who took the opportunity to get closer to John again.

Jacy was back with my Bleu Tropique. I looked up and saw that Dan and the French girls had disappeared and that Emma and Mark were now sitting together with a bunch of saddos. I think they were discussing exam results.

I already felt slightly lightheaded from my share of Jacy's first Bleu Tropique. I decided to take this one slowly. Now the crowd had thinned out a bit, Jacy sat opposite me. Becky and John moved apart a little too. Becky probably wanted a part of the Jacy action. I didn't mind. I didn't consider her to be competition exactly, and I wasn't quite ready to be alone with him.

Becky went in to bat for me. 'It's good that Sophie's recovered so quickly, isn't it?' she said to Jacy.

Uh-oh. I didn't want to be reminded that less than twenty-four hours ago I was throwing up *fruits de mer*. 'It was nothing,' I chimed in. 'I'm just more sensitive to the sun than I thought I was. It's not as if I burn. I just go brown.'

'That's why that white dress looks so gorgeous on you,' said Becky loyally. 'And it shows that your legs go up to your armpits.'

I didn't want her laying it on too thick, but I drank some more Bleu Tropique and found I didn't really care. It was great just to have Jacy there, admiring me. I opened my mouth to say something coolly dismissive but no real words came out. 'Hic!'

'Pardon you!' said John.

'Hic!' came out again.

Jacy looked concerned. 'Drink a bit more. Drink it slowly,' he said. I did. But it had no effect whatsoever on the hiccups. They just got worse. Becky was no help. She just dissolved into a heaving mass of giggles beside me.

'Girls, eh?' said John to Jacy. He pronounced it 'gairls'. Becky was throwing herself around now. 'Watch out! I'm getting a face full of your hair!' He pronounced it 'hurr'! But Becky had had it. Tears streamed down her face. Every time I went 'Hic!' she heaved her large body around. Her giggles were infectious. To me, at any rate. I started to giggle as well as hiccup. I kept trying to drink slowly from my glass, but it only seemed to make matters worse.

'What shall we do with 'em?' said Jacy to John, as Becky and I leant against each other helplessly.

'I'll get this one back to her caravilla,' said John. 'It's almost next door to mine. And you (yer jammy feller),' he added under his breath, 'had better do the honours with Sophie.' He pulled Becky to her feet and guided her out through the main bar.

'Bye Sophie,' she snorted. 'Don't do anything I wouldn't do!' she added as she and John swayed off into the night.

Jacy had a quick word with the girl at the bar while I tried to stop myself from falling over. Then he put his arm round me. 'Easy does it, Sophie.'

'Hic!' I replied.

'Ssh! Most people have gone to bed.'

Through my haze I felt flattered and a little anxious at the same time. Was Jacy making a move on me? Could I cope? The rain-washed air smelt of wet pine. The moon had risen above the trees. I concentrated on putting one foot in front of the other, all the time intensely aware of the warmth and strength of Jacy's arm.

'Here we are,' he said when we reached our tent. 'Home in one piece.'

'Thanks Jacy.' I smiled up at him, staggering slightly as he gave me a little push towards the tent.

He reached out and ruffled my hair. 'All part of the service,' he said, and set off at a jog back to the bar.

I unzipped the tent as quietly as I could. I needn't have bothered with the stealth. Danny was sitting at the table with a cup of coffee. 'Hi!' he whispered. 'What have you been up to?'

'Jacy walked me back to the tent,' I said.

'Ooh-er.'

'He got me rather drunk,' I added, knowing that Dan would agree that that meant Jacy was seriously interested in me. I threw myself onto a camp chair, remembering with pleasure the strong arm around me and the affectionate hand in my hair.

'What on?'

'Don't tell Mum and Dad!'

'Your secret's safe with me! They're next door with Emma's mum, anyway.'

'That blue drink. Bleu Tropique, or whatever. I feel really squiffy.' I giggled. 'And it gave me the hiccups.'

Dan looked at me. I realised he had a condescending smile. 'Bleu Tropique has no alcohol in it whatsoever, Sophie. That's why the couriers drink it when they're on duty.'

Six

'Dad, can I have the money to hire a bike?'

'I'm surprised you've managed so long without one. Here's the money. Bring me the change.'

'Great,' said Becky. 'Let's go and get one for you now.'

It was twelve noon and I hadn't been up long. I'd lain awake for a while thinking about Jacy and what last night meant, but I didn't come to any earth-shattering conclusions. I could still bring back the memory of the hairs on his warm arm around my shoulders and the surprise of his impulsive gesture when he ruffled my hair. But I preferred to forget the embarrassing 'effects' of the Bleu Tropique. Now at last the holiday seemed to be falling into place, thanks to Becky. And here she was, dragging me off to hire a bike.

She wheeled hers as we set off for the Acceuil. As soon as we were out of earshot she said, 'Well?'

I looked at her.

'You tell me about Jacy before I tell you what a good kisser John is. Go on! What happened? You're so lucky! How romantic! I knew Jacy was perfect for you!'

'You – and John? You pulled?'

'Yes! We went and sat down by the lake for a bit. He's nice. I like him. But I told my dad you were with me, so you'll have to cover for me if he says anything. But go on! I want to hear about you two!'

I was tempted to fib a bit. But since last night seemed to be a stage on the way to true romance I decided to tell it how it was. After all, it had felt romantic at the time. 'Well, he did put his arm around me. He didn't seem to mind anyone seeing us. And then he walked me back to the tent—'

'And then?'

'He – er – he sort of ruffled my hair!'

'Wow! I'd give anything to have Jacy ruffle my hair!'

'Hey! What about John?'

'Oh, that's just a physical thing really. You and Jacy are far more exciting!' She whispered that because we had come to the Acceuil. The French girl, Hélène, was on reception. I knew her English was hopeless but I just said 'Bike?' and made pratty bicycling motions. She giggled and Becky stepped in.

'Elle veut louer une bicyclette pour – how long Sophie? – dix jours.'

'Oui, bien. Ca sera soixante-dix francs, s'il vous plaît. Choisissez.'

'Give me the hundred note,' said Becky. 'Here's thirty change. Come on, let's find you one that works! Merci! Au revoir!'

'Bye!' I muttered.

'Now we can check out the horses.' We cycled off together. Becky on a bike was quite a sight. She wore Levi shorts which were definitely not a good idea and a sleeveless Nike top. She was all thighs and elbows and big hair. But it was a great way to whip up a breeze and keep cool in the midday sun. We pedalled along the road at the top, past the entrance to the manoir, the shop, the table tennis area and the pool to the far end where the stables were part of the old farm. We turned into a courtyard with a square of green in the middle shaded by four tall trees. Around the sides were stables with horses looking out over the doors. There was a slightly whiffy farmyard-in-the-sun smell and hens scratching about. A couple of dogs lay panting in the heat and a group of girls stood in the shade chatting.

I wouldn't have known where to begin, but Becky went straight up to the girls and sorted everything out in French. It was impressive, this side of Becky. I haven't met her parents yet but I imagine that she has a marvellously large and efficient mum.

'That's all fine,' she said, getting back on her bike. 'We just turn up here tomorrow morning at ten o'clock. They'll kit us out with hats and boots – and horses I dare say – and off we'll all go. Back about five. Bring a packed lunch, plenty of water to drink and two hundred francs and Bob's your uncle!'

She picked me up again after lunch on her way to the pool. Dan had gone on ahead with Emma and Mark. Becky wore her shorts over her bikini, but we were still treated to ample amounts of flesh on view. I don't mind swimming and sunbathing in a bikini but I'm not quite ready to put myself on show to the whole world. I was wondering vaguely where Jacy was today when he appeared from the bar as we cycled past. 'Hi girls!' he said.

'Wow! Did you see the way he looked at you?' Becky practically swerved into me.

It seemed to be accepted that the teenagers colonised a square of grass by the fence at the end of the pool. There was quite a large group already there as we flung our bikes down. We spread out our towels and before long John and Steve joined us, along with three Kates, two Jamies, a Lauren, a Tristan and a Melanie. Steve and John had an amazing repartee going – very funny and very quick. I could never have joined in their rapid-fire jokes and one-liners – they were like stand-up comedians on the telly. At first I couldn't even work out what they were saying, but after a while I got used to them. The accent was all part and parcel of the humour. They were different from anyone I'd ever met before, but I liked them. Steve was the older and bolder of the two. John was his stooge. Most of their jokes were about themselves, too. They didn't mind drawing attention to their zits and their white bits, bits that needed shaving, unruly bits. Becky joined in sometimes. She made jokes about being fat and having periods. I couldn't believe it. She wasn't embarrassed about herself. She didn't mind talking to the boys about the bits of her that were less than perfect. And believe me, there were plenty of them. I mean, I'm happy with my looks. I could do with bigger boobs and better nails, but I couldn't joke about it.

'Hey, Sophie, you like the fellas, don't you?' Steve asked.

'Course she does,' said John. 'She likes us, doesn't she?'

'Well, we know Becky likes us,' said Steve, nudging John.

'I like you,' I said. 'I think you're funny.'

'Did you hear that, Steve?' said John. 'She thinks we're a bit of a "larf" –' he took the mickey out of my accent.

'I heard,' said Steve. 'You've got a treat tonight, girls.' He addressed the Kates and Lauren and Melanie as well as us. 'Because the Irish are coming. We met them at the last campsite and a whole lot of them are coming on here today.'

'That should keep the couriers busy . . .' said John. (So that's why Jacy wasn't around much.)

'And if you think we talk funny –' said Steve, 'just wait till you hear them.'

'Would you like an ice-cream, like?' It was Mark. I tried to put the thought of 'ice-cream' before 'irritation' and smiled graciously.

'Yeah, we'd like ice-creams, Mark. Do you want a hand?' Becky didn't have the same problem as I do with

Mark. 'Can you cope with la belle Hélène or do you want some language support?'

'Got some, thanks,' said Mark as Suzette appeared at his shoulder. She had a pencil and some paper.

'Cassis pour moi,' said Becky. 'Double.'

'And vanilla for me, please.'

'Chocolate,' said John.

'Rum and raisin for me,' said Steve.

'Pay me when we get back,' said Mark.

'Ah, this is the life, eh?' Steve rolled over luxuriously. 'That Suzette can bring me all the ice-cream she wants.' He sighed lasciviously.

'Steve!' Becky slapped him resoundingly. 'You just keep your lewd thoughts to yourself, OK? There are women present.'

'Just commenting on the local beauty, that's all,' said Steve, cowering.

'Yeah, Steve!' said John, putting an arm round Becky. 'Put a sock in it.'

I decided it was time for a swim. I couldn't keep up with all this backchat. I walked off to the pool and dived in. Steve followed me. I swam a few lengths crawl and then one in backstroke. The trouble with backstroke is that you can't see where you're going. I bumped into Steve at the shallow end. I stood up spluttering. 'Spit on me, would yer?' he laughed.

'Sorry!' I wiped my face with my hand.

'I know you're a bit too high and mighty for the likes of us, Ms Morris,' said Steve as I ducked my shoulders under water, 'but, you know, there's one of the Irish lads that you'll find impossible to resist. All the girls just love him. He's called Fergal.'

'Fergal!' I said, splashing him and diving out of reach. 'What sort of a name is that?'

*

At suppertime Becky and I cycled back to our tent together. Her brother and the twins came to meet us. They looked hot and excited. Two of the Dutch boys were with them. 'Jacy's been training us for the big match!' they said. 'He's brilliant. He played for his county when he was at school in England.'

'He's so cool!'

'He's brilliant in goal!'

'He can shoot too!'

'He scores every time!'

Emma was behind us with Mark and Dan. 'What a lot of fans Jacy has,' she said. I didn't like her tone.

I don't believe it! Drippy Emma actually thinks she stands a chance with Jacy herself. When Becky and I went into the bar after supper we found them poring over a sheet of paper together. She looked so guilty! They both stood up when we came in. Jacy folded the piece of paper and said, 'Don't worry Emma. Whatever happens, we'll make it a night to remember.' Then he turned to us. 'Girls!' he said. 'Can I get any of you a drink before I go and sort out newcomers?'

Emma had disappeared. At least she knows when she's outclassed. 'You go and sort out newcomers,' said Becky. 'Then you'll have all the more time to spend with us later!' He skipped out with a wave and Becky grinned at me triumphantly. 'You didn't want another Bleu Tropique did you?'

The bar was unusually empty, but there was quite a commotion outside. Becky and I bought our drinks and sat up at the bar itself where we could watch what was going on. Several cars had just arrived and a large number of people had clambered out of them. They were stretching their legs and shaking their shoulders as people do after long journeys. Steve and John and some of the others were also in there somehow and the whole crowd started hugging and high-fiving with a large amount of noise and good humour. Campers carrying saucepans of frites stopped to look, bikes skidded to a halt, dogs yapped and there was a general carnival air. So this was the great event. The Irish had arrived. I scanned them surreptitiously for a gorgeous bloke and listened out for the name Fergal, but none of them caught my eye half as much as Jacy who was also in among them, trying to find out who was going where. Now and then he cast mock despairing glances in our direction at the bar and I melted, memories of his hands in my hair making me come out in goosepimples all over.

The scene at the bar never really got going that night. Some of our friends came in to buy cans and bottles, but it was too nice an evening to be indoors, and it seemed that the bonfire at the lake was going to be the main attraction. People were drifting over there already.

Becky didn't want to go down yet. 'Wait a bit,' she said. 'Then we won't get roped into building the fire. Anyway, it's much better when it's darker.'

'That's fine by me,' I said, seeing Mark and Emma, my brother and the French girls heading in that direction. I was more than happy with my grandstand view of Jacy in action.

'I want to stop off at the caravilla on the way down,' said Becky. 'Cover myself in insect repellant and find something with long sleeves. I got bitten to pieces down there last night.'

She caught my eye. 'By mosquitoes! And I don't want a repeat performance.'

'Not any of it?'

She gave a rueful laugh. 'I'm not bothered,' she said. 'I don't mind if John wants to, but I shan't be heartbroken if he doesn't. I don't have much experience with blokes, but the one thing I do have experience of is of them going off me. It's probably because I'm fat. They don't want their friends to see them with me.'

'John didn't seem to mind this afternoon.'

'That was just mucking about.'

She was right. But how bleak. My problem was the opposite. Boys don't give up on me. They ring me late at night and tell me they love me, and they blame me and call me a bitch – and worse – for not reciprocating. Maybe that's bleak too. Why do we bother with boys at all when they always make our lives a misery one way or another? But then I caught a glimpse of Jacy sprinting past again and remembered precisely why. I'm not sure that I've ever felt like this about anyone before. I don't think I've ever met anyone so gorgeous. Oh Jacy.

'Enough of this!' said Becky. 'Let's go to the caravilla.'

The prairie at this time of night was like a comfortable suburban street. Blue smoke rose from the barbecues. Adults sat around with bottles of wine, chatting, reading, playing cards. Little children batted around in their night clothes. A game of boules was in progress – elderly Frenchmen in swimming shorts fought it out with a group of white-blonde young Dutch girls. It was idyllic in a way. Becky's caravilla was a long way down. I could see why she needed a bike. Her brother and the twins were sitting over a Gameboy and I recognised her father reading a paper at the table.

'Hi!' said Becky, stepping up into the caravilla. 'I've brought Sophie back, Mum.' I followed her and saw, not the large lady I'd been expecting, but an amazingly beautiful forty-something *slim* version of Becky. She looked like the sort of woman who spent a lot of time at the gym.

'Nice to meet you, Sophie,' said her mother. 'Are you on your way down to the lake?'

'Any crisps I can take, Mother, or chocolate?'

Her mum laughed indulgently. 'I was just the same at her age! You never stop eating, do you Becks? Look in the cupboard, darling.'

Becky opened the fridge first, took out two cokes and slid one across the table to me. 'Have this, Sophie, while I get the anti-mozzie stuff. Do you want to borrow a blouse?'

I certainly wanted to check out her wardrobe. 'OK.' She had a tiny little cabin to herself in the caravilla – with its own wardrobe. She threw open the door.

'Help yourself.'

Wow. It could have belonged to Eddie Monsoon! There were even some *Lacroix* jeans! I didn't know you could even buy them in a size 14! I picked out a flimsy blouse, another of her Kookai numbers, that I felt comfortable with. 'How about this one?'

'Whatever.'

'Thanks. It's gorgeous.'

'I'm sure Jacy will go for you in that!'

I wasn't so sure. It was lovely having Becky being so full of romantic ideas and egging me on, but I had a nagging little doubt, unfamiliar to me, that maybe Jacy wouldn't go for me in anything. I've never felt so insecure. I just needed another sign from him that he thought I was special.

Seven

We walked down to the lake in the twilight armed with a torch, a large bottle of coke and loads of crisps. We both smelt strongly of insect repellant. It was more overpowering than Becky's Tommy Girl and my Issey Miyake.

Where the path through the woods opened out into the field by the lake we could see that the bonfire was already well under way, rosy flames competing with the sunset and its reflection. There were about thirty teenagers silhouetted against it. The crackle of burning wood, muted shrieks and giggles blending with the aggrieved honks and quacks of waterbirds drifted over to us. It was magic. Becky squeezed my shoulder. 'Good, eh?' We used our stuff to set up a little base of our own near the bonfire and sat down. 'This is just so perfect. All we need now is for Jacy to come down, row you into the middle of the lake, take you in his arms and SNOG you . . .'

She practically sang that bit. Thanks Beck. It drew a crowd, too. 'Did somebody use the word "snog"?' It was Steve with John (looking sheepish when he realised precisely who had used the word) and four more guys. 'I told the lads they had better meet the posh birds at the earliest opportunity,' he said.

'We're not posh!' Becky and I said in unison from where we sat.

'Well, you talk posh,' said John.

Becky and I made 'What, us?' expressions at each other. Then Steve pushed the four Irish lads forward to introduce themselves. They stood there looking embarrassed.

'Sit down,' said Becky. There was a large log near us and they perched on it in a row, like four hunched crows in their hooded tops.

'I'm Sean,' said the first one. (He really said 'Oi'm.')

'I'm Peter,' said the next one, 'his brother.' (Brother rhymed with bother.)

'I'm Gus,' (he pronounced it 'Goss') said the one with the little beard. 'Their older cousin and superior in every way!'

Then they all turned to the one on the end, the one with the copper curls and eyes so blue you could drown in them, who said, 'And I'm Fergal Maguire. No relation.'

I didn't know people spoke like that for real outside Father Ted. I felt the bubble of a giggle rising up in me, but Becky dug me sharply in the ribs with her elbow. 'Hi,' she said. 'I'm Becky and this is Sophie. So where are you from?'

'Dublin,' (Doblin) they chorused.

'Oh wow!' said Becky. 'I just love your accents. I could listen to you all night.'

'You shall, my darling, you shall,' said Gus and took a swig of his beer. John suddenly appeared at Becky's side.

'Let's go on the lake – there's a couple of pedaloes free.'

'Brilliant idea!' said Gus. 'Come on Steve, Peter, Sean!'

'There's only room for four,' said Steve. 'Take Fergal instead of me!'

'Don't worry about me,' said Fergal.

'You and Sophie come with us, Fergal,' said Becky.

'You can pretend it's Jacy,' she whispered to me, as the boys went ahead of us.

The boats were pretty mucky – I was glad I wasn't in a white dress tonight! Fergal was the perfect gentleman. 'Would you be wanting to sit on my sweatshirt?' he offered as we clambered onto the rocking boat.

I looked at him to see how serious he was. He had folded his lanky frame into the corner of the seat and was grinning shyly at me. 'I'll be fine, thanks.' I smiled back at him. He was cute.

Becky rocked the boat a lot as she sat herself at the pedals. 'Whoa there!' yelled John, trying to keep the thing level.

Becky yelped. 'I'm what you call ballast!' she laughed. 'A boat needs weight!'

John sat at his pedals and whooped. He enjoyed himself with Becky, I could see. He liked the person underneath the flesh, and I admired him for that. They gradually co-ordinated their efforts and moved us out onto the lake. The four boys on the other pedalo were doing far worse. For a start, they couldn't decide who was going to pedal, and nearly capsized the thing as they argued over who was to sit where.

'Would you look at them! That's the marvellous thing about you women,' said Fergal. 'You have a civilising influence, so you do.'

'Doesn't take long for the charm offensive to begin!' said John. 'Take no notice, girls, he can't help it!'

'I like it,' said Becky comfortably.

We were moving quite fast. I dabbled my hand in the shattered water and pretended Fergal was Jacy. I imagined it was just the two of us out there on the lake. The sky was inky blue with a sliver of a moon. In the distance the fire leapt and danced. People moved around like shadows at a distance. Jacy and I were removed from all of them. He stroked my hair. He moved closer, cupped my face in his hands and looked deep into my eyes with that melting gaze. Then we kissed.

CRRUNCH! 'We've been rammed! This is war!' It was John. 'Come on Becky, *pedal*!'

Steve, Sean, Peter and Gus were like little boys, grinning and yelling, 'Tee-hee! Gotcher!' as we went spinning out of control.

But John and Becky were up to the challenge. They pedalled us out into the middle of the lake at amazing speed and lined themselves up to ram the others. 'Wey-hey, I love it!' said Fergal. I was sad to let go of my daydream but this was a gas. I knew it was the sort of thing Jacy would have enjoyed too. I threw myself into yelling and splashing with the best of them. We all got soaked. I hope Becky's blouse wasn't ruined. At six-four to us we headed back for shore. A small crowd had built up there wanting their turn, including my brother and Emma and the French girls. (Why Emma, Dan, I thought, when you could have Suzette on a plate?)

We climbed out – Fergal offered his hand to help Becky and me down, would you believe – and ran over to the fire to warm up a bit. We clutched our bottles and cans and crisps and got as close to the flames as we dared. The boys were chucking things on the fire as boys will, so Becky and I moved to one side. 'I know he's not Jacy, but Fergal's a bit yummy, isn't he?' she said.

'That's the thing, though, he's not Jacy. Honestly Becky, I think I'm going mad! I can't think about anything else. I just wonder what he's doing, and whether he's thinking about me. I'm not interested in anybody else. Fergal's a bit young. And – ' I made sure she could see I wasn't too serious, ' – he *is* a ginge.'

Becky had seen that I wasn't serious, but for the first time in our friendship she looked at me witheringly, in a way that made me uncomfortable. 'Sophie Morris! Does *everyone* have to be perfect in Sophie-Morris-land? You'll be saying you don't like fat people next!'

'*You're* not fat!' I lied unconvincingly and braced myself for the weight of Becky's scorn.

'So that's OK, then.' She emptied her can of drink and crushed it vehemently.

I wanted to make amends. 'I'm *so* sorry Becky. I seem to be getting it wrong with everyone this holiday, and I really don't want to get it wrong with you. I know I must seem a bit superficial. Perhaps I am.'

She didn't rescue me.

'Well, I know I have been up until now. But I can see I've been immature—'

'Don't grovel, Soph. We're cool. But even fat people have feelings. Hey!' she broke off. 'Look over there! It's lover boy!'

I saw him at the end of the path from the woods, just a white T-shirt in the dark, but unmistakably lithe and *Jacy*. 'He's waving!' I said, delighted. We waved back. But someone else was waving from the water. Someone else was climbing out of a pedalo and running to pick up a torch. It was Emma who became a bobbing will o' the wisp of torchlight, moving through the dark to where Jacy stood, and Emma disappearing up the path to the campsite with him.

Becky grabbed me. '*No*. It's not how it seems. Emma and Jacy, no way. That was about something else, something to do with them in the bar earlier. I swear, Sophie, that those two do not have a thing going. But we must make a cunning plan for you, Sophs.'

'Do you still want to?' I felt crestfallen on two counts.

' '*Course* I do. When we go riding tomorrow, that's what we'll do. We'll plot and plan and work something out. I still think you're so right for each other. It will be so romantic.'

'Am I forgiven, then?'

'What for?' said Becky, laughing at my forlorn expression.

The rest of the evening at the lake was great, despite the turmoil in my head. People drifted around. Some smoked, some drank, a few couples sneaked off, but for most of us it was just friendly and undemanding. Gus was one of the ones who drank and made a noise. Steve kept him company. Fergal sat in the glow of the fire gently playing someone's guitar. He seemed to be playing more for himself than the crowd, but I could tell he was pretty good. When it was late, John came and found Becky. I didn't see her putting up a big fight when he persuaded her to go with him. I decided it was time to go back and felt relieved to see Dan and the French girls coming towards me on their way up. Mark was with them. 'Coming, Soph?' Dan reached down a hand to pull me to my feet and I felt ridiculously grateful that my big brother was being nice to me. Mark was speaking desperate Geordie French, which Francine and Suzette loved, so Dan and I led the way with the torch. 'Good down there, isn't it?' he said, not really wanting an answer.

Just before we reached our tent Francine and Suzette came out with a torrent of French that I couldn't understand, though I judged by those cutesy smiles that they wanted something. 'They want us to take them back, because we've got a torch,' said Mark.

'Oh yeah!' said Dan, laughing. 'OK girls, we'll protect you against strangers in the night, won't we Mark? See you later Sophie.'

I could hear Dad snoring inside our tent. It was dark. I stumbled around, looking for the hurricane lamp. Suddenly there was someone standing there. I drew in my breath ready to scream, but he put a hand over my mouth.

It was Jacy! 'Don't scream,' he whispered. 'You'll wake everyone up! It's only me.'

'What are you doing here?' I asked.

'Oh, just hanging around waiting to catch the lovely Sophie Morris alone.' He laughed softly. 'Sorry if I frightened you. Bye!'

Was that the sign I'd been waiting for? I just didn't know.

Eight

'What do you think all that was about, then?' I asked. Becky, inelegant in the extreme on a bike, knew what she was doing when it came to sitting on a horse. I was already a bit uncomfortable, being chafed in places I didn't even know I had, and we'd only been going about twenty minutes. Twelve of us followed two leaders round the far side of the lake into pastures new. It was another beautiful hot day, but a light breeze was going to make the heat bearable.

'Do you really think he was waiting for me, Becky?'

'I suppose we're going to have to come to terms with the fact that he'd been next door with Emma.'

'I just don't see it.'

'We don't know why he was with Emma. They're planning something for sure, but I can't even think what they might have in common. I mean what could "a night to remember" possibly be?'

'I don't care, as long as it's not a romance. Jacy wouldn't have such poor taste!'

'Emma's all right. I don't really see what you've got against her—'

'Her dress sense for a start!'

'But she fancies your brother, doesn't she?'

'I don't know any more. It's just that, whatever the reason, I refuse to believe that Jacy fancies her. OK, then, let's assume Jacy had come from there. But why did he say he was waiting to catch me alone?'

'Typical male, isn't it? To assume that you'd be on your own. I suppose he must know you like him, and because he's so sure of himself he couldn't imagine there being any competition.'

66

'But he's right. Nothing compares . . .'

Becky started singing, 'Nothing compares, no-*thing* compares with you . . .'

'Well, they don't. And I do like him, so why would he mess around? You don't think—' I was about to express my doubts when Becky cut in.

'I KNOW!' she shouted. 'THAT'S IT! You've got to pretend there *is* competition. It never fails to pique the male ego. That's what we've got to do. Sophie. Make him jealous.' Her horse sensed her excitement and started to canter about a bit. She reined him in.

'Do I want to make him jealous? What if it backfires on me? What if he's been having a thing with Emma all along and I never realised?'

'Of course you want to make him jealous! If he thinks you're interested in someone else he'll be there to stake his claim before you can say "Jack Robinson"'.

'I suppose it might move things on a bit. I've been here since Monday, and it's Friday now, so it's time something happened. Well, time a bit *more* happened. He did walk me back to the tent on Wednesday and he did surprise me last night. I keep thinking one thing is going to lead to another, but it never does.'

'That's because blokes are lazy, and if they don't have to try then they won't. I expect he just takes it for granted that you'll be there for him whenever he decides to make a move on you.'

'A bit how I felt about him, really.'

'Then perhaps THAT explains last night! Perhaps he was trying to make *you* jealous! He's probably waiting for you to make the first move!'

Becky had a point. And I desperately wanted to believe her, even if my gut instinct was to be less convinced. Her explanation also made sense of his behaviour. It was so unlikely that he really was after Emma, but he'd made sure I saw them together.

'OK Becky. So how do I go about making him jealous?'

'I'm working on it.' The two of us had fallen behind the other riders, so we thought we ought to catch up. We were trekking through the trees where it was beautifully cool. It was no hardship to canter after them – the horses' hooves thundered satisfyingly on the forest floor. We met up just before our route took us along a sunbeaten lane that wound its way between fields of sunflowers. The sun blazed down on us as we took to the road. The riders – people of all ages from nine to sixty – went quiet in the extreme heat. I looked at row upon row of sunflowers all turning their faces to the sun and I thought – *Jacy is my sun. I want to turn my face to him wherever he goes. When he isn't there I want to close my petals and sleep until he appears again. If he were to leave me now I know I would shrivel and die*. A poem started to form in my brain to the rhythm of the horses' motion, but it was only the last lines, *If you were to leave me now, I know I would shrivel and die*, that kept on repeating themselves.

At last we turned off onto a bridle path that was shaded by tall oak trees. It was bordered by blackberry bushes, and we leaned down to pick a few early ones. 'Let's stop for a minute,' said Becky. 'I need a drink of water.' She glugged down half a bottle, screwed on the cap and said, 'Right. I've thought of our plan. The main problem is, who do you make him jealous with? There's Mark, of course—'

'I think not, Becky, not even for getting Jacy.'

'Well, I could lend you John. Or there's Steve. He fancies you.'

'No way! Does he really?'

'John thinks so. Could you pretend to fancy him?'

'I don't think so. He's just not my type.'

'Nobody's asking him to be. Remember what this is in aid of!'

It was no good. I couldn't contemplate lowering my standards even as a ploy. I cast my mind over the boys I'd met in the last few days. One of the Jamies wasn't too bad. At least he was taller than me and had a good tan. And though Tristan was a bit of a boffin and wore a brace, I found his brain quite appealing. But they still didn't meet the Sophie Morris impeccable requirements.

Becky burst in on my ruminations. 'What about the Irish lads?'

'What about them?'

'They're nice.'

'They're Irish.'

'So what? Sean and Peter are quite good-looking. And Gus is a laugh.'

'I can't understand a word they say. And Gus is too noisy.'

'There's always Fergal Maguire.'

'Why d'you say his whole name like that?'

'Because its such a wonderful romantic name. I think he's lovely.'

I kept quiet about the 'ginge' reservation. In fact it didn't really apply any more – I'd caught sight of Fergal outside the shop this morning and seen that the colour of his hair in daylight was the most extraordinary dark foxy red, the henna colour all my friends dyed their hair a couple of years ago.

'Maybe.'

'Go on, go on, go on!' she said in her best Irish.

'OK. And suppose I do use Fergal, how do I go about it?'

'This isn't something I've ever done myself, you understand. But from watching other people I think the idea is to give Jacy the eye all evening, and then, just when he's interested, you head for Fergal as if you'd been together all along.'

'If Jacy's interested, I'll want to go along with it. No, the best way to make someone jealous is to pretend you don't care but make sure they can see you with the other person, or be able to overhear you when you're talking about him. Fergal would have to be in on it. Otherwise he might react all wrong.'

'Sounds as though you're an expert. You don't need me!'

'Shut up!' I attempted to swat her – not easy on horseback. 'I'm so scared that it won't work. I'm really crazy about Jacy, Becky, I don't think I've ever felt like this before. I was so sure he'd want to go out with me – other guys always do. And he's so nice to me, he makes me feel special.' I couldn't tell even Becky just how much I was in love with Jacy. This was something even I wasn't used to. I mean, imagine wanting to write poetry about him! Me, wanting to be a sunflower! I'd definitely got it *bad*.

'Exactly. So what you need to do is to be all touchy-feely with Fergal so that Jacy can see what he's missing. I'm sure I'm right, so don't argue. We'll ask Fergal tonight. You can start in the bar. We'll make sure you're sitting next to Fergal and Jacy's bound to see you – he always comes in to the bar at some point. I sometimes wonder if he's got something going with the girl behind the bar.'

'No. Hélène's got a French boyfriend somewhere. Suzette told my brother when we first arrived.'

'OK. So you're all chatty with Fergal in the bar where Jacy can see you. Couriers don't usually come down to the lake, so you can just be normal there. Then tomorrow there's Karaoke night. And the couriers organise it so they'll have to be there. We know Fergal can sing OK – you'll have to do something sloppy together, some old thing like *Especially for You*. They always have that one.'

'OK, OK! Don't go too fast. Let me get used to the idea. Anyway, it looks as though we're stopping for lunch.'

*

It was a relief in some ways to climb down off our horses. I felt as though I'd be stuck in that position for ever. This was obviously their usual stopping place because there was a rail for tethering them and a water trough. We were at the top of a hill with a view down over the way we had come. We could see the campsite in the distance with the lake and the forest and all the toy-sized green and yellow tents among the trees. It felt as though we were looking at the Earth from the moon – a whole little holiday world down there full of people going about their holiday business, cooking, swimming, playing, falling in love. I wondered what Jacy was doing at this moment. Probably something mundane like cleaning out tents. Jacy even managed to make pulling a cleaning cart full of Flash and disinfectant look glamorous and noble. There I was again, *turning my face to my sun.*

'Oy, you!' Becky intruded on my daydream. 'Mum's given me far too much food. Do you want a peach? Or a yoghurt? Or a bunch of grapes? Or some chocolate? Sometimes I think she wants me to be fat! Do you know, she says she was once like me, but it all fell off when she left school. So there's hope for me yet. I might be as skinny as you one day.' She laid into the chocolate.

When we had finished eating, the guides called us all together to look at the view and point out where we were going on the homeward trek. They spoke in French so it wasn't much use to me, or half of the other people on the ride. Becky translated some of it for me. I'm beginning to think I should work a bit harder at French at school. It's humiliating not being able to understand anything even though I've been learning for three years.

We packed up our bags and got back into the saddle. The horses were a bit grumpy at first, but then they realised we were on the way home and got into line.

71

Becky and I were up at the front this time, me following her. The guides, two girls of about nineteen or twenty, were gossiping – in French of course. Naturally we didn't take much notice, but then the name Hélène kept cropping up. Becky concentrated on listening. She dropped back a bit to report. 'I can't quite catch what they're saying, but it's something to do with her boy-friend – how they never get any time together. It's not as if we've ever seen her with a man, is it? I'll see if I can find out who it is.' She moved closer again, but fell back soon after. 'They're not talking about her any more now. They've moved on to football – "le football"! Shame. I like eavesdropping when people think you can't under-stand what they're saying.' We trotted on. I was in front this time. I tried listening in. Becky was right. It was all 'le football' – and that's boring even when you do under-stand.

We clattered into the campsite at about four. We could hear the shrieks coming from the pool as we rode past the far side of it. 'Don't you just long to dive into that cool water?' Becky asked.

'Swimsuits would be good,' I said. We walked rather agonisingly back to my tent. Mum, Dad and Dan were still out in the town.

'It's all right for you,' said Becky. 'I've got to cycle on with a sore bum to my caravilla to get mine.'

'I'll wait for you,' I said. 'I want an ice-cream, so I'll change and then meet you at the bar.'

'OK. See you in about twenty minutes.' Becky struggled on to her bike and pedalled off wearily. I was tempted to spend the time jotting my poem in my diary but some-how the thought of a shower was even more appealing. It was lovely to smell of shampoo and body lotion rather than horse and sweat. I put a pair of shorts on over my bikini, pulled a comb through my hair – it was only going to get wet again – and wandered over to the bar for *une double – vanille et cassis, s'il vous plait*. No time like the present for improving one's French. GET A GRIP SOPHIE! I reminded myself. Poetry and learning French? What was going on here? The words 'sad' and 'geek' came to mind. I pushed them away, smiled back at Hélène – she was laughing at my French really, but her gorgeous smile was irresistible – and attacked my ice-cream.

It was dark inside the bar. I was about to make my way into the bright sunlight outside when someone called me. 'Did you not see me over here, Sophie? We've been lookin' for people all afternoon, but we've not seen them. It's good to see you, so it is!'

Fergal.

'Hi Fergal. I'm meant to be meeting Becky outside, but I suppose she'll see me when she comes in to buy an ice-cream.' I sat down at his table. 'Where are Gus and Peter and Sean?'

'They went back to the tent to play cards. We don't spend all our time together, you know. I wanted to find out where everyone else was.'

'I was like that when I arrived,' I told him kindly. After all, I was going to be asking him a BIG favour pretty soon. 'The way it works here – for teenagers like us, that is – is sleep in the morning, pool in the afternoon, bar after supper and lake after that. Most days, that is.'

'So what are you doing here now?'

'Becky and I went riding for the day. It was great.'

'Won't that be costing a lot?'

'My parents paid.'

'Oh,' he said. 'That's nice.'

There was a short silence. I sensed I'd said something slightly odd. 'That's what parents are for, isn't it?' I asked with a laugh.

'I wouldn't know. I don't have parents,' he said shortly.

'Oh God, I'm sorry. Have I put my foot in it?'

'No. My mother died when I was very little. She was just a girl when she had me, so my grandmother and grandfather are like parents to me. I don't know my father. I think he was a student at the University, but my mother never told and he never knew about me.'

My ice-cream was melting. I licked it round the edge to stop it dripping while I thought about the turn this conversation was taking. I felt it needed booting into the present. 'Who's brought you here?'

'Sean and Peter's mother and father. They're teachers. They often bring Gus – he comes from a very big family, and this year they offered to bring me too. Me and Peter have been mates since juniors. But we don't have to do everything together. I like to be on my own sometimes.'

Becky burst in at this point. 'My God! Sophie! Don't tell me you're chatting up an Irishman?'

'Why not?' I asked, aggrieved.

'Why shouldn't she chat up an Irishman?' said Fergal, his face lighting up with amusement.

'Sophie doesn't do Irish. Or French. Or Geordie. She just about manages Scouse though, don't you Soph?'

I wasn't sure I liked this. 'I understood every word Fergal said,' I protested. Then I realised that this sounded worse than ever. They were laughing too loudly to hear me trying to make amends.

'See what I mean?' said Becky, guffawing.

'I obviously spoke very slowly and clearly!' said Fergal, but he gave me one of his nice grins.

'I'm trying to be better,' I said feebly.

'Good,' said Becky. 'Let's go for a swim. Coming, Fergal?'

'How could I refuse?' he said, untangling his limbs from the chair and table. 'It just so happens that I have my swimming gear right here.'

*

'Becky!' I hissed. We were playing on the flume in the children's pool. Fergal had just gone down ahead of us. 'You're going to have to ask him. I don't know what to say.'

'Perhaps you won't need to say anything. He seems pretty keen already.'

'Exactly. I told you – he has to know what's going on or he might not do what I want, and blow it. Please, Becky. Please say something for me.'

'I love it when you beg. OK. Don't worry. I'll ask him.'

'Tell him that Jacy and me are virtually going out – we just need a little help. But make sure he knows that I'm in love with Jacy. Exclusively. I really need him to know that. At least – I think I do. He has to be told I'm in love with Jacy, doesn't he Becky?'

'Stop wittering and leave it to me. I'll get to the bar before you do tonight and corner him.'

'You won't let Jacy hear, will you?'

'What sort of idiot do you take me for?'

Nine

It all went very well. I don't know exactly what Becky said to Fergal, but I sat next to him in the bar, and when Jacy put his head round the corner I quickly looked adoringly at Fergal and squeezed a little closer to him. I caught Emma giving me some funny looks, and Mark some doleful ones, but they didn't bother me.

Down at the lake we just had a laugh. We really were singing round the campfire (memo to self: DO NOT tell the folks back home about this one). Fergal borrowed Mark's guitar and got us all going. He has a great singing voice. That's going to be useful because singing has never been my strong point and I'll certainly need him to be confident if we're going in for the Karaoke. It felt as if we'd all been there forever – me, Becky, John, Steve, the Irish contingent, my brother, Emma and Mark, the French girls, Tristan, Jamie and all the others who formed our group. I had to admit I was enjoying myself. Having a great holiday even. Except of course for Jacy.

I bumped into him this morning at the shop. I tried to compose my face to look uninterested, but how could I, when he was in swimming gear, a towel round his neck and drops of water still running in a delicious line down the middle of his chest and clinging to his hair. At least this time I was presentable. I'd had a shower and was wearing shorts and a top that showed off my tan.

'Sophie! Hi! Sonia and Coralie made me buy breakfast today so they could have a bit of a lie-in before the Saturday rush begins. What brings you here so early?'

I couldn't sleep for thinking of you. You shine like the sun. Are you jealous yet? I don't know what to say. 'We needed – ' I looked into my basket. It contained two plastic bottles of semi-skimmed milk and some bubblegum – 'stuff.' Well done, Sophie. I looked at him helplessly.

'Fine. Good. Right – see you later, at the Karaoke tonight?'

'Yes please.'

Oh *God*! He wasn't in*vit*ing me! He was just reminding me that it was on. Too late. He'd gone. I cycled back to the tent.

Becky was waiting for me – she was up earlier than usual too. 'Do you want to come to the beach with us?' She was panting – she'd obviously cycled fast. 'My brother's invited the twins and Mum and Dad said I could bring a friend. There's plenty of room in the Volvo.'

'I'd love to. I have to get away from this place. I've just done something so cringe-making! Let me give these to Mum and then I'll come.'

'We'll pick you up in about twenty minutes – no rush!'

'There is for me. I really want to do a disappearing act right now.'

'I'll make sure they don't hang about.'

Dan wasn't up yet. Dad and Mum were having coffee – hence the milk (OK, so I was being a helpful little girl to my loving parents for a change, but I wasn't going to tell Jacy that).

'Did I hear you were off to the beach, darling?' said Mum.

'If it's all right with you.'

'Of course it is. I don't know what Dan's up to, but I think he said something about football, so I imagine you're not interested.'

'No interest whatsoever Mum.'

'Are you going to the Karaoke after supper?'

'We were thinking of it.'

'Jesse mentioned it to us – it seems it's for everyone – us oldies as well as you.'

'Jacy, Mum. Jacy.'

Becky's family rolled up in their Volvo. They tooted and the twins shot out from the tent next door, scattering beach towels, goggles and bodyboards in their wake. I followed rather more sedately. Becky's car had three rows of seats; her parents sat in front, Becky and I sat right at the back facing the other way and the three boys sat in the middle. That meant we could chat without being too bothered by their incessant football talk, interspersed only with awful songs and chants. 'My brother has nothing whatsoever in his mind apart from the match on Monday night,' said Becky.

'What match is that?' I asked.

'WHAT MATCH?' said all three boys turning round together.

'That's what I asked,' I said, laughing at their incredulity.

'Only the England v. France match at the campsite,' said one of the twins.

'Haven't you seen the posters?' said the other.

'Can't say I've seen any posters,' said Becky mildly, and we carried on talking about my embarrassing encounter with Jacy.

'Mum said he told them about the Karaoke evening too,' I said.

'And did your mum say "Yes please" like you did?'

'It wouldn't surprise me! She fancies him too.'

'At least it means he'll definitely be there. Which gives our plan a better chance of working . . .'

A Karaoke night might sound naff to you, but all I can say is that, when it's with a group of friends and there isn't any alternative entertainment, it's actually pretty cool. Our lot went to the bar first and rolled up at the crêperie where the younger kids were already up on stage doing their stuff. It wasn't so much a stage as a raised platform with stairs at either side at one end of the room. There were French windows all the way along so we could hang around outside and still hear. It was mostly parents and younger children inside, but I remembered that most of the little ones were dragged off to bed at about ten. We found the list of songs. They were all old favourites with a few corny French songs thrown in, but we signed up as a group for 'YMCA' and 'Bohemian Rhapsody'. Tristan was being very organised at this point and telling us what to do. 'Male solo here – where's Fergal?' Fergal loped over. 'I'm putting you down for "When I Need You", Ferg. And there's some male/female duos here too.'

'Only too happy to oblige,' said Fergal. He looked down the list. 'You'll do one with me won't you Sophie – something from *Grease*? That will be some crack!'

Now, if there's one film I have watched at least a hundred times, it's *Grease*. I know all the words off by heart. 'Which song?'

' "You're the One that I want".' He grinned. 'We can do a bit of a dance as well.'

'I'm on.' I know all the steps, too, so maybe my less than brilliant singing voice won't be so apparent.

Coralie and a huge bunch of kids were doing one of those songs with loads of actions. Everyone was joining in, including us. I looked around for Jacy but he was nowhere to be seen. He'd better be there for my romantic duet with Fergal, I thought. Singing in public is not something I take on lightly.

'YMCA' was the next song to come up. An extremely large group of us crowded onto the platform, so many that it wasn't possible for all of us to see the screen. You know 'YMCA' – all you really need to do is fling your arms about to make the letters at the right time, so I didn't really care about the screen. 'Young man . . .' the intro started. I could see Coralie and Sonia marshalling troops for the next song. It seemed to be a gathering of campsite staff. Surely Jacy would be among them? I peered at the far doors – there he was!

'Y–M–' I sang as loudly as I could and threw my arms into a Y. Oops. The intro was repeating. Damn. I should have known that. Everyone else was singing 'Young man' again – and those around me were starting to giggle.

'Now!' whispered Becky with an exaggerated nudge. 'Y–M–C–A!' I was trying to concentrate, honest. I threw my arms out again, in Becky's face this time. By now everyone was laughing. We were a riot. We had every-one joining in. In fact the only people not joining in were the campsite workers as they prepared to do their rendering of 'Summer Holiday'. They filed up the stairs on one side of the platform as we toppled down the other and fell outside to let our excitement subside. The others whizzed off to buy drinks but I wanted to watch 'Summer Holiday'. Jacy, Coralie and Sonia were on stage, but so were the campsite staff who worked in the bar, the restaurant and reception, the *guardien* and even the owners who lived in the manoir. Madame had a wonderful operatic voice. It was quite a line-up. They were brilliant and had the whole audience in stitches. After it, Madame gave a little thank-you-and-welcome speech which was also the cue for parents to take the little ones away. Jacy had disappeared again so I lost interest for a while. Fergal wanted to run through the *Grease* steps in a corner of the courtyard. Yes, we went all the way through the dancing part, skips, 'ooh ooh oohs', dirty dancing and all.

'Hey! You can dance!' he said as I strutted my Olivia Newton-John stuff. So could he! John Travolta eat your heart out, I thought, but I didn't say it. 'I hope you can manage to sing as we dance – I'm not sure I can do both.'

'It's the singing I'm not so sure of,' I told him. 'I know the words and the steps. I'm just not so confident about coming in on the right note.'

'Don't worry,' he said. 'It's only a laugh! I've got to go back in again now and make a fool of myself with "When I Need You".'

'I'll come back in and listen.'

'I'll sing it just for you then!'

Steady on, I thought, but then, what better way to make another guy jealous? I found myself in a crush with the gang – Becky and John, Steve and Gus. 'Hit them with it Fergal!' yelled Gus as Fergal made himself comfortable with the mike and the intro started up. Fergal looked over in our direction, and then – he was really playing his part well – he fixed his gaze on me and began singing.

'Wow!' said Becky. 'He's fantastic!'

'I know,' I said. 'I almost wish he was doing it for real! *Someone* can't fail to be jealous!'

Becky looked at me blankly. Then understanding dawned. 'Oh! Yes! Jacy. Yes, I bet he'll wish he could sing like that.'

The roar of applause that came at that point was deafening, but my pleasure in the ruse was short-lived. Jacy was going on stage again. Jacy, Madame et Monsieur, Hélène and – *my parents*! Oh my God, what was going on? Dad had his arm round Hélène's waist and was grinning like a moron. Mum was in between Monsieur and Jacy and, likewise, grinning like a moron. *CRINGE*! Dan looked wildly over at me, eyes popping and eyebrows working overtime. 'I don't know!' I mouthed back at him as I saw him block his ears. That wasn't enough for me. I covered my eyes with my hands.

'Haw-hee-haw-heee-haw-haw-haw . . .!' It was a French song – 'La Vie en Rose'. Mum and Dad have never done anything as embarrassing as this before. Dad kept looking at Madame and squeezing Hélène's waist instead of looking at the screen so his words just sounded like a donkey braying. Mum was the opposite. She glued her eyes to the screen and stood stock-still, so the others all bumped into her as they swayed from side to side in true Gallic fashion. It was a nightmare. I wanted to die. What would Jacy think of someone with such idiots for parents?

Everyone else was laughing uproariously. How could they! I realised I was standing with one hand in front of my eyes and the other over my mouth when Fergal tugged at my arm. 'Come on. It's us next.' So there we were going up on stage as the French songsters went down the other side to great cheers of approval. The audience thought they'd been *funny*! Clearly a case of alcohol-fogged judgement. Our lot gave Fergal and me a clap. I had the satisfaction of Jacy looking back at us as he made his way down into the audience and hearing someone shout 'Break a leg!' – though actually I think that was Mark. Still, they were on our side. I struck my funky-Sandy pose, and we were off.

'Sandy!'

'Tell me about it – stud.'

And then Fergal was John Travolta. He did those amazing hip waggles, screamed, fell down – everything.

'You'd better shape up . . .' There wasn't much stage but I managed to skip about. Then I had the inspiration to skip down one side of the stairs so I could skip up the other. It worked really well and Fergal seemed to anticipate what I was doing all the time.

'You're the one that I want! Ooh Ooh Ooh!'

I got up the stairs again for my next verse and Fergal managed to fall down them convincingly after he'd said 'Wow!' but we somehow managed to synthesise our dancing for the duet at the beginning of the long last chorus. It was going so well.

But then disaster struck. I danced down the stairs again – and toppled – right over into the audience. My ankle was agony. I clutched it and looked up at the stage. Fergal was carrying on. He was singing and dancing as if I was still there! He ran his hands up and down my imaginary body and kept his eyes on my imaginary face. People were transfixed. I tried to stand but my ankle was too painful. I sat down on the floor again. Mark was at my side. 'I saw you fall, Sophie. I saw you fall.' He put my arm round his neck and helped me up. 'I'll get you some first aid. I'll get you some first aid.' He hopped me over to Sonia and Coralie.

'Jacy's our first aid man,' said Coralie. 'He went back to be on duty at our tent while we were all here.'

'I think I've only sprained it,' I told her. 'But it really hurts.'

Mark said, 'Can you move your ankle? You're sure it's not broken?' I wiggled it around. It hurt, but at least I could do it.

'Jacy might have company,' said Coralie to Mark as this was going on. 'Make lots of noise as you approach.' I was in too much agony to wonder why lots of noise should be necessary. She turned to me, 'But he'll bind up your ankle for you, Sophie. He's a dab hand with a bandage.'

Mark helped me out as all my friends leapt on stage for the last song, 'Bohemian Rhapsody,' led by Tristan. There was no way I could have joined them. Being this close to the odious Mark was almost more than I could handle, but to be honest, my ankle was killing me. I even felt a teensy bit grateful to him for helping me when all the others were in thrall to Fergal doing our duet singlehanded. But most important of all – I was on my way to Jacy!

If he said 'Are you all right (a' reet), like?' once he said it a hundred times as we made our way along the road at the top to the couriers' tent. 'I thought you sang great, Sophie,' he said. 'I thought you sang great. You and Fergal are great together.'

I was going to butt in before he could repeat that statement, but we were right by the couriers' tent and I thought it wouldn't hurt if he said that nice and loudly. He did. 'You and Fergal are great together. Hello?' Jacy wasn't in the office bit, but he emerged from his 'inner' tent, a courier's only refuge, looking slightly less cool, calm and collected than usual. From singing with my mum, I expect!

'What's up?' he said. 'Oh hi, Mark. Hi Sophie.'

'Sophie's sprained her ankle. Sophie's sprained her ankle.'

'So Sophie's sprained her ankle has she?' said Jacy, with a mischievous smile at me.

'Sonia and Coralie said you might be able to bind it up for me.' I didn't want him thinking it was my idea.

'OK,' he said. 'Now let's have a look. All good training for doing medicine next year.'

'I'm hoping to do that, too!' said Mark.

Well, well, well, who would have thought it, I found myself thinking, but most of me was concentrating on my foot in Jacy's hands. And that took some concentration. He twisted it gently in both directions. 'Does this hurt?'

'Yes!'

'Does this hurt?'

'Yes!'

'I think you're right. It is only sprained. If it was broken you wouldn't be able to move it.'

'That's what I said,' said Mark.

Jacy went to a cupboard with a big blue cross on it and took out a roll of bandage. 'Mark, could you just pour some cold water into that bowl? Thanks.'

'This might not be very professional Sophie, but I can probably do this best if you rest your leg across my knee.' If my ankle hadn't been so painful I would have been in heaven.

'Thanks Jacy. You're being –' I tried to catch his eye '– amazing.' That wasn't quite what I meant to say, but it's certainly what I felt as my throbbing ankle was deftly bound in wonderful cool bandage.

'There. How's that?'

I stood up. I was able to stand up. Great, I'd be able to get back to the tent without Mark's help. Maybe, if I could get him to go, I might get a chance to thank Jacy properly . . . 'Great. It's much less painful. I can get back on my own now, Mark.' I looked meaningfully at him, hoping he'd take the hint and leave me alone with Jacy. He didn't. 'I'd like to thank Jacy, Mark.'

'Thanks Jacy, man. Thanks.'

'I'd like to thank him. Personally.' I glared at him.

'Oh. Ah. I'll wait outside. I'll wait outside.' He shambled off.

Jacy looked at me, puzzled. 'No big deal, Sophie. It's all part of the job.' He cast a glance towards his 'inner' tent. 'I'll be catching up on my beauty sleep now.'

I stood there. I wanted to throw my arms round his neck and thank him for making me better. I wanted to say he could hold my feet and bind my ankles whenever he wanted. I wanted to tell him I loved him, that I was doing all that stuff with Fergal for show. I tried to look in his eyes. 'I—'

'—You comin' Sophie?' Mark put his big head round the tent. 'You comin'?' The moment was lost. Quick as a flash I gave Jacy a peck on the cheek.

'You were wonderful, thanks.'

Outside I could barely contain my anger at Mark's ineptitude. 'Don't you know when to leave people on their own?' I hissed. 'Jacy and I wanted to be alone. For your information, we've been waiting a long time to be alone together.'

'I'm sorry. Sorry. I thought he – you—'

'Well you were wrong. Of course, someone like you wouldn't understand the meaning of sexual attraction—' I felt thwarted and furious. Dim old Mark couldn't stop putting his foot in it. I didn't care what I said to him.

'Sophie,' he said mildly. 'I can see why all the girls fancy Jacy. I can see why. But you do know—'

'Nothing that *you* can tell me,' I said rudely. We had reached our tents. I was aware that people could hear us. 'Well thank you for your help. Goodnight Mark,' I said as dismissively as possible. Mum and Dad were inside the tent. Dan was no doubt out and about, but I wasn't up to larking around the lake. I didn't want to have to do my act with Fergal again, not when there was no possibility of Jacy seeing us. I couldn't understand why I had messed up that opportunity so much. If only Mark hadn't been hanging around. Effing Mark. I could hear him now.

All cheerful. 'Hi, Mum! Hi, boys! That were all good fun, weren't it?' Funny how he didn't repeat himself with his family.

I sat down at the table and lit a couple of nightlights. I put my foot up on one of the chairs and remembered Jacy's firm touch. It was a while before I noticed a note tucked under Mum and Dad's wine bottle. It was a piece of folded paper with SOPHIE written on it. I opened it: this is what it said:

I feel a weird affection that I'm too shy to convey.
So I guess I'll just meditate in your direction, and be
  on my way!
Fergal
PS Where did you go?

It was just a verse from our song. Why had he bothered to write it out?

Ten

Mum was very solicitous in the morning. She unzipped my compartment. 'Poor old Sophie! You *are* in the wars! Let me have a look at your ankle. We were right the other end of the room and by the time I got to the stage I heard that Mark had taken you off to the couriers for first aid. I was waiting for you, but I'm afraid I fell asleep. You should have woken me.'

'I was OK. Jacy bandaged it for me.'

'Let me have a look.' The ankle was a bit swollen but not too bad. The cool bandage had obviously done the trick. 'I'd like to see you walking on it before I pass judgement. It's quite late, darling. Why don't you get up and have a shower? Dad and I want to go to a service in the village church and I'd like to know you're fit enough to leave behind.'

'Of course I am, Mum. But I might as well get up.' I wanted to be fully prepared for visitors. Fancy being crocked twice in one holiday! It really isn't like me. I quite liked the idea of reclining on a sun lounger in my bikini and holding court. I hobbled off to the shower block. It was still quite painful to walk, but I could tell that I was already on the mend.

I put my dressing gown on over my bikini and sat down for breakfast. 'Well,' said Mum, 'and what did you think of me and dad last night? Stars, eh?'

I started to um and ah, the very thought of their little performance still bringing me out in goosepimples, but luckily she interrupted me. 'I thought Fergal was marvellous. And you too, darling. He carried on so bravely when you disappeared. A difficult decision I should imagine – whether to stop and see how you were or carry on.'

I thought about Fergal. I'd been quite impressed with him carrying on too. It hadn't occurred to me that it might have been nicer of him to find out if I was all right. But then Fergal wasn't anything to me. I wasn't bothered. And there had been that strange note . . .

'Eat your croissant, darling.'

Dan stumbled out, blinking in the bright light. 'Morning all. You and Fergal were pretty cool last night

Sophie. Especially when you fell over. We all had a good laugh!'

'Thanks, brother.'

'Did you hurt yourself?'

'Yes, as a matter of fact. But Jacy did first aid on it, so it's not too bad.'

'Jacy? He'd make any girl feel better.'

Mum grinned over at Dad. 'Just as Hélène would make any man feel better, don't you think, Giles?'

Dad looked sheepish. 'Well, she's a very lovely girl.'

'Thank goodness that was our one and only Karaoke night,' said Dan. 'Go on, you two. Go to church and confess your sins! I've got yet another football practice. They're working us very hard for people who are meant to be relaxing.'

'One more thing before we go,' said Mum, 'We've been invited next door for a barbecue tonight, so don't go making any other plans.'

I anointed myself with suntan lotion and made myself comfortable on the sun lounger with a Walkman and a pile of postcards. I thought it was time I sent some. I wrote to Hannah first. I wanted to tell her about Jacy. She's my friend so I had to be honest – I just put, 'There is the most gorgeous goodlooking courier here, and I think it's only a matter of time . . . I've made some good friends. Weather good. Hope your music thing goes well.' For Charlotte I just wrote 'Hi, wish you were here.' Maddy's was more difficult. Maddy expects men to fall at her feet, and mine for that matter. So I fabricated just a bit. 'I'm having a holiday romance with the most gorgeous goodlooking courier. Tell you all about it when I get home.' (None of these quite tallied with the more anguished truth that was reported in my diary, but hey! I had to keep my end up in the holiday romance stakes. They expected it of me.) That was all for the time being. Mum had put stamps on them earlier – they might even reach England before I did. I suddenly found myself thinking about Ben Southwell. For the first time in my life I had an inkling of what he'd been feeling. Perhaps I should send him a friendly postcard. After all, we were going to have to see each other when school began again. But it could keep. He was probably still on holiday himself. In France, what's more. I remembered reminding him that France was a big place when we discovered we were both coming here – especially as he was going south and I was going west. I'd been pretty foul to him.

'Sophie!' That accent was unmistakably Irish.

'Hi Fergal!' I held up his note and waved it about. 'What was all this about?'

'I – I – er – I just wondered what had happened to you last night. One minute you were falling off the stage and next minute I couldn't see you anywhere. I didn't know whether or not to carry on, but, you know, the Karaoke machine is so relentless, and I was caught up in it. I'm so sorry. I really should have checked you were OK but I didn't know what to do for the best. I wanted to apologise.' He was quite distressed.

'Don't worry. I was fine. Jacy did first aid on my ankle.' I gave him a knowing smile.

'Jacy? Is that a French courier?'

'No, silly. He's English. You *know* . . .'

But he wasn't listening. 'About the note. It wasn't meant to embarrass you. Forget it. Anyway, I came to say we're off to the beach all day, but see you tonight, OK?'

'Wait! Why should I have been embarrassed? They were just the words from the song, weren't they?'

'Well yes, almost.'

'And I'm afraid we're having a barbecue next door tonight, so we won't be coming to the bar.' I grimaced at him, to show how I felt about the barbecue, but he was still looking confused when Gus came down and said, 'Come on, lover boy. We haven't got all day. See you later, Sophie!' and dragged him off . . . JUST in time to cross paths with Jacy. This was more like it!

Jacy had his cart, but he left it up by the road. 'How's the ankle?' he called, though he stopped briefly and said to the two boys, 'Are you two coming to the football tomorrow?'

'Our problem is that we don't know whether to be English or French!' said Gus.

'*Your* problem!' laughed Jacy. 'No one minds, mate, it's just a matter of making up the numbers! Come if you can! Though I warn you, the English have been practising!' He came over.

I propped myself up on my elbows. Then I suddenly remembered the postcards and turned them picture-side up. I wondered if Fergal had spotted them. 'The ankle's fine, thanks to you,' I said with an enticing (I hoped) smile. But then I suddenly felt nervous about being alone with Jacy. I'd made a conscious decision to wear my bikini – the pale blue one that showed off my tan – but now I felt exposed.

'I see your singing partner came to enquire after your health before I could!'

'Fergal?' Now I was stuck. Should I play the jealousy game and say how natural it was for Fergal to visit me, or should I be truthful and convey that Fergal meant nothing to me, compared with him?

'Who else?' he said. 'What a voice! That guy could do it for money!' Ha! He was jealous already! I didn't have to play games. 'Now are you lying there looking beautiful because you can't walk or because you can't help it?'

Wow. What a lovely thing to say. I realised I was making Bambi eyes at him. He had another stab. 'Is your ankle still too painful to walk on? I can only do first aid, you see, I'm not qualified to follow it up. But we could get you to a doctor if it's bad.'

'Oh.' I twigged. He was here as a courier not as a courtier.

I got to my feet and limped towards him. He held out his hand ready to support me when I reached him. I was tempted to stumble so he could pick me up – my knees felt weak enough. But then – interrupted again! It was ratty little Sonia with her cart. 'Come on Jacy! Stop chatting up minors! We've got four caravillas to clean out by lunchtime and I'm not doing them on my own!' I'd never liked her.

Jacy gave me a rueful smile. 'Slave labour, that's all we are. But it seems to me that you're on the mend, Sophie. OK Sonia, I'm coming.' He caught sight of my postcards on the ground. 'Do you want me to post these, since you're immobilised?' He bent down and picked them up.

'NO!' I shouted, terrified.

'Censored stuff, are they?' he said, still smiling. 'Don't worry, I won't read them,' and walked off to pull his cart alongside Sonia, my postcards in his back pocket.

I couldn't run after him. I lay back, sweating. I tried desperately to remember what I'd written. I hadn't put his name, had I? Mum and Dad always say that messages on postcards are public property – an excuse for reading ones addressed to me, I reckon – but this was different! I'd said 'a courier', hadn't I? And he was the only male courier. I know! I could pretend they were Dan's postcards. That was it. I'd get Dan to thank Jacy for posting *his* cards and to say he hoped he hadn't read them. My mind was racing. No. I couldn't do that. I'd signed them. I could pretend that I thought Fergal was a courier. A motorbike courier! I could ask Jacy if he knew that Fergal was a really good motorbike courier as well as a good singer. Nope. Oh where was Becky when I needed her? Of course, Jacy might be flattered! The postcard to Hannah wasn't so bad. But Maddy's. What had I said? 'I'm having a holiday romance with a gorgeous goodlooking courier'? Depends how you define romance, I suppose. Perhaps he wouldn't be able to read my writing. Perhaps he really wouldn't read them at all, like he promised. No. Everyone reads postcards. Aaaagh!

Mum, Dad and Dan all came back soon after, but nothing could really take my mind off the postcards. I had to admit, I would be totally mortified if Jacy read them. I couldn't convince myself that he would be flattered. All I could do was pray that he hadn't read them, or that he'd passed them on to someone else to post.

My prayers were answered, but not quite in the way I'd expected. Becky came over after lunch and I decided I was up for a swim, so I limped along to the pool beside her. We were walking past the couriers' tent when Sonia called me over. My heart sank. I'd told Becky about the postcards. 'Uh-oh,' she said. 'Tell her it's none of her business. Whatever it is.' And she hung back while I hobbled over to see what Sonia wanted.

She was looking more ratty and pointy-nosed than ever and her glasses had an evil glint. 'Just a word, Sophie,' she said. I felt as though I was at school. I saw that she had composed her face into a sympathetic expression. 'I know it's none of my business,' she began. (Too right, I thought.) 'But Jacy gave me your postcards to post. Now I don't normally read postcards, and I honestly wasn't intending to read yours but what you'd written sort of leapt out at me and I thought I ought to put you straight.' Oh my God, she'd seen the one I wrote to Maddy. I couldn't speak. 'The courier, Sophie, is already spoken for.'

'What?' I said, rudely. What was she on about? Why couldn't she speak English?

She gave a smug smile. 'He already has an attachment to –' she paused, '– another member of staff.' She lowered her eyes meaningfully. 'I just thought you should know. In case – you make a fool of yourself.' My God! She meant herself! She was telling me that Jacy was attached to her! As if! What was she playing at? 'Don't take it too hard,' she said with a patronising look. 'Just a friendly word of advice.' She retreated into the couriers' tent.

I stared after her for a minute before hobbling back to Becky in high dudgeon. 'The cow!' I said. 'I always knew she was a cow. As if she could make me believe that Jacy fancied her.'

'Excuse me?' said Becky. 'Calm down. Take some deep breaths and tell Aunty Becky everything.'

I told her.

'Who does she think she is? I always thought she was like a school prefect. And she shouldn't have read your postcard. What a witch. Ignore it, Sophie. Just be glad it wasn't Jacy who read it.'

'That's a point. At least he doesn't know. Though I wouldn't put it past her to tell him.'

'What, and let him know that someone a million times more beautiful than she is fancies him? No way. She'll want to keep him for herself. I don't think she'll tell him.'

'Thanks Becky. You're great.'

'Fat, but great.'

'I'll ignore that. I'm learning a lot on this holiday.'

'I'll say.'

I tried to hit her, but for once she was too quick for me.

The Irish boys left a big hole in the swimming party. Perhaps it was because Gus was so noisy. My brother was there but Mark and Emma, embarrassingly, were shopping with their mum for the barbecue in the evening. Francine and Suzette had Dan to themselves. They were doing wonders for his French – and his street-cred! So we were more sedate than usual.

Becky wanted to know more about last night. She said how everyone was talking about Fergal's singing and dancing. I felt ever so slightly peeved that no one was talking about my singing and dancing. I thought I had been pretty good until I skipped off stage. But I had to keep my thoughts to myself with Dan and Becky around. I thought I'd just bask in some of Fergal's reflected glory – since he'd made a point of singing at me.

'Tell me about Jacy bandaging your ankle,' she said with a sigh. 'Lucky you.'

'He's going to medical school after the summer,' I said.

'So the boy has brains as well.'

'Apparently Mark is heading that way too,' I said cautiously. I was feeling a bit worried about Mark after last night.

'Oh I knew about Mark,' said Becky. 'He's something of a genius according to Emma.'

'Mark?'

'Oh yes. Straight "A"s.' She paused to let that one sink in. 'By the way, Fergal was really worried about you last night. He was in a real state about carrying on when you'd hurt yourself. How did you end up at the couriers' tent?'

This was a difficult one. 'That's the point. Mark took me, actually. Sonia and Coralie told him to.'

'Mark?'

'The very same. Anyway, Jacy bandaging my ankle was fabulous – all sort of firm but gentle.'

'Wow. He wouldn't have been like that with just anyone.'

'I wanted to, you know, like, *thank* him, properly, but Mark got in the way.'

'Jealous, probably!' She laughed. 'Mark being jealous! Now that's not what we planned, is it?'

'Talking of our plan – Becky, what exactly did you say to Fergal? You did tell him that I was in love with Jacy, didn't you? And that my liking him was all a fake?'

'It's not *all* a fake, is it?'

'I like him OK, of course.'

'Only *like*?'

'Becky! Did you or did you not tell Fergal about my feelings for Jacy?'

She was still hedging. 'Trust me! He was very willing to pretend to like you. I'm hot. Come in to the water and cool off.'

I was not looking forward to the barbecue. I don't like Emma. I don't like Mark. The twins are irritating and I don't know their mum. When Dan and I got back from the pool we could smell the charcoal burning. The rest of my family were in the tent when Mark came over to say, twice, that they'd be ready in half an hour. He was all spruced up in a clean T-shirt and wearing aftershave. 'Whatever,' I said, feeling bored at the mere thought of it, and went into the tent to tell the others.

'Yes,' said Dan. 'We heard. And we heard your reply too. Now just be nice for once. It won't hurt you. They just want to be friends.'

'Oh yeah. Mark because he fancies me and Emma because she fancies you. And their mum because she probably fancies Dad.' I stuck my chin in the air defiantly.

Suddenly Mum was on my case. 'SOPHIE!' she roared, and it frightened me because she's usually very mild, my mum. She linked her arm in mine quite viciously and dragged me off down a path that leads to the washing lines. We walked in total silence. When we were out of earshot of everyone she laid into me – verbally that is.

'Sophie Morris. You are behaving like a spoilt little brat. I don't know what's eating you these holidays but I'm not proud of you. You boss poor Becky around and you're foul to Mark. You're rude, snooty and, quite frankly, plain horrible some of the time. I haven't liked some of the things I've heard you saying to Danny one bit. Now, you're my daughter and luckily for you I get to love you however you behave. But other people won't. Other people notice, you know. If you're unpleasant to Mark it reflects back on you eventually. Some of those boys you fancy won't like you any better for acting like a bitch.'

'Mother! How dare you call me a bitch!' I felt my mouth trembling.

'I'm not calling you a bitch, darling, but you've been bitchy, there's no denying. I don't like to interfere, but I also don't like to see my precious daughter letting herself down. You owe it to yourself to be liked for who you are as well as how you look.'

I cried. 'I'm sorry, Mum, I just get so fed up with droopy blokes.'

'That's not a good enough excuse I'm afraid, Sophie. I'm not about to lay a guilt trip on you, but you must realise that that family is not having an easy time at the moment?'

'Aren't they?'

'Has it escaped your notice that one member of their family is missing?'

'Well, no dad, but loads of families don't have dads.'

'And do you think that makes it any less hard for Mark and Emma? Not to mention their mum?'

'OK, OK. You said you wouldn't lay a guilt trip on me.'

'I just want you to look at the world around you a bit more.'

I rolled my eyes. 'Give me a break, Mum.'

Oh dear. I'd gone too far. 'SOPHIE!' she shrieked. And she carried on shrieking. 'OK. I'll play dirty too. You're sick of droopy blokes. Well, I'm sick of a droopy daughter. I don't know who you're mooning about after, and I don't care, but it strikes me that you need a taste of your own medicine. You don't deserve to have people falling in love with you, you really don't.' She looked unforgivingly at my tearful face. 'Right. I'm going back to that tent and I expect to see you there, looking nice, five minutes before we go next door. OK? Because if you can't behave yourself I can't enjoy myself, and we'll pack up and leave tomorrow. I mean it. So get your act together. Stop being so immature. And if you manage to do that you'll restore some of my respect for you and we can carry on as before.' She strode off.

I sank down on the grassy bank where she had left me. I couldn't stop crying. Mum had been shouting so loudly, people must have heard. The couriers were out and about at this time. Sonia might have heard. Or Jacy. Oh my God, what if Jacy had heard? Was I drooping about? I suppose I was, a bit. But to say I didn't deserve to have people fall in love with me – that was savage. Perhaps I simply didn't deserve Jacy? Was that it? I started crying all over again.

This wouldn't do. Mum, incidentally, is perfectly capable of carrying out her threats. I made a terrible fuss about going round to some family friends for lunch once and in the end Mum said she'd cancel them, even though we all knew that they would have made the meal and everything. She rang up and said she was very sorry but we weren't coming because Sophie was being so impossible. I was mortified for weeks because the daughter was a couple of years ahead of me at school and she told all her friends.

I tried to pull myself together. I wanted to tell myself that Mum had been unfair, but enough had happened on this holiday already to make me realise deep down that she wasn't. I do find it easy to despise people – Emma for her clothes, Mark for his looks, people who talk funny, fat people, ginger people. That word 'immature' stuck in my mind. Might someone despise *me* for being an immature person?

I looked at my watch. I had five minutes to get to the shower block, wash away my tears and show up at the tent. I ran (hobbled extremely fast would be a better description) for the shower block as if I had chronic diarrhoea so no one would stop me, and locked myself in a cubicle. I splashed cold water all over my face and through my hair for a couple of minutes. I looked in the mirror. I didn't look too bad. A bit like the romantic heroine in a film when her lover has just died. I smoothed back my hair into a topknot and headed for the tent. Mum was waiting for me. She didn't say anything but gave me a really big hug. I nearly cried again, but now wasn't the time. I was going to be NICE.

'Hello everyone.' Mark and Emma's mum, Mary, had changed into what can only be called a 'frock'. Stop it Sophie, there I go already. Emma had put on tons of eye make-up – I say nothing, and even the twins had brushed their hair. OK, in my new caring mode I must give them names: Matt and Harry.

'Smells delicious,' said Dad. Actually, it did.

'It's bound to be,' said Mum. 'Mary's a cordon bleu cook.'

'Was,' said Mary. 'And cordon bleu isn't much use at a barbecue! Now, what's everyone going to drink? I'm assuming that your two will drink wine with us? We are in France after all. Or we've got some beers?'

I glared at Dan. 'On your life,' I whispered. I did not want him saying that I managed to get drunk on drinks without any alcohol. 'Coke would be fine for me,' I said with my sweetest smile.

'I wasn't offering drugs,' said Mary.

I looked at her appalled.

'Joke!' she said. 'Sorry Sophie. Fish a coke out from the cool box, Mark. What about you Dan? A beer?'

'Great,' said Dan. 'Why don't you two give us booze?' he asked Mum and Dad.

'Because then there wouldn't be so much for us,' said Dad. 'Personally, I look forward to sharing a pint with you when you're eighteen, but we're not at home now, and when in Rome, you know.'

'All families do things differently,' said Mum.

I began to worry that we were being a bit rude. Mary was only being hospitable. But she didn't seem to mind at all. She was knocking back her gin and tonic pretty quickly in fact.

We filled our plates with food that was indeed excellent. Emma had made all sorts of salads and Mark was very efficient with the barbecue. The twins handed stuff round and Mary kept everyone's glasses filled. Well, she certainly kept her own full. By half-way through the meal Mum and Dad kept putting their hands over their glasses.

Emma, Mark and Dan were all quite easy with each other. I even felt a bit left out, sitting by Matt and Harry. They were eating with great gusto and talking loudly about, guess what, the football match. OK Sophie, I thought, TALK to them about it.

'Right, you two. Now I know absolutely zilch about this football match tomorrow. Tell me all I need to know. One at a time.'

'Well,' said Harry. 'It's England v. France. And it's tomorrow night at seven p.m.'

'And Jacy's been coaching the England team.'

'But Emma's the captain.'

'And not all the English are English—'

'And not all the French are French—'

There are quite a few women playing—'

'And the French are wearing blue T-shirts—'

'And the English are wearing white ones.'

'And we're going to win!'

'Because Jacy and Emma are top!'

I blenched. They'd lost me some time ago but this statement brought me up with a jerk.

'So have the captain and the coach worked, er – *closely* together on this?'

'Oh yes. They've planned their team and their strategy, tactics, that sort of thing . . .'

So THAT was what Emma and Jacy had been up to. It was so simple. He didn't fancy her! He wasn't trying to make me jealous! Harry shrunk from my sudden interest. Matt leant over to him.

'Mum's at the bottle again, stop her.'

Harry got up and I saw him simply remove the bottle of wine from his mother's elbow and start offering it around. It was a practised move. 'More wine anyone?'

'Well, why not?' said Dad obviously aware of the situation and with a glance at Mum as if to say, I'll do this to help out but you'd better stay sober.

Mary got up to get the next course and promptly tripped over a guy rope. She swore roundly. 'Oops, sorry everyone.'

Quick as a flash Emma was at her side. 'Sit down and

enjoy yourself, Mam. I'll serve it. Are the fruit kebabs done, Mark?'

'Yes. You just get bowls and cream and I'll deal with these.'

The fruit kebabs were gorgeous. I've rarely tasted anything so delicious. And that, added to my discovery that Emma and Jacy had only been planning football together, made me full of beneficence. 'They're amazing!' I said, and smiled at Mark. He smiled back, hugely, enormously, a never-ending smile. I held it. I saw all manner of mood changes and colour shifts pass through his grey-blue eyes. I thought, yes I really did: you poor bloke. Dad gone and your mum making a fool of herself and being the oldest and a family holiday and OK, falling in love with me, and you have to hold it all together, all on your own. I was still feeling raw emotionally myself and tears started to prick at my eyes. I looked down. 'Really yummy,' I said.

'Thank you,' said Mark.

Mary was talking to my parents about sex. They were both pinned back in their seats, unsure whether to laugh or not. Mum did, she pretended that everything Mary said was enormously funny. Dad stood up. 'Mark, lad. Let's you and I have a game of pool. Dan can wash up. You've done enough.' I was aware, with a marvellously secure feeling, how Mum and Dad and Dan were coping with a tricky situation, just as Emma and Mark and the twins were. Nothing was said explicitly but all of them were sensitive to what was going on around them. I was impressed, and even a little humbled.

Possibly for the first time in my life I said, 'I'll help with the washing up!'

'We don't want to break up the rest of the party quite yet,' said Emma gently – she wasn't putting me down – looking over towards our mothers. 'I'm really sorry about this,' she whispered. 'It doesn't happen very often – well, not that often. I'm going to pack the boys off to the table tennis tables or somewhere, if that's OK with you. They seemed to have you rapt back there!'

'They were telling me about your football match tomorrow.'

'Blimey!' said Dan. 'I never thought I'd see the day!'

The twins were more than happy to leave us. 'Back by eleven, please,' said Emma to their departing backs.

'It's going to be a good match,' said Emma. 'Jacy's playing for us, but the Irish lads are playing for the French. Fergal's ace apparently.'

'That will make up for Suzette, then,' said Dan. 'She's detrmined to play, and as we've got Emma and a couple of other girls Suzette thinks there should be at least three women on the French team.'

'Haven't you heard all this, Sophie?' said Emma.

'No. It's amazing what you block out when you're not interested. And as Becky isn't interested either we haven't a clue what's going on.'

'But you talk to Jacy, don't you?'

'Er, yes.' Was this a trick question?'

'She thinks Jacy fancies her!' said Dan, suddenly getting his own back.

Emma laughed. 'I shouldn't think so!' she said. Then, 'Don't worry Sophie, I won't let on!' And she and Danny laughed some more.

My good intentions went straight down the pan. 'You patronising cow!' I yelled and speed-hobbled past Mum, who was helping Mary out of her chair. I hurled myself into our tent. Where I sobbed my heart out.

Eleven

'Mum says I've got to apologise for upsetting you. I was only teasing but she told me she heard what I said and that she can understand why you flew off the handle, especially after she'd just had a go at you. So, sorry. OK?'

'You can take a breath now.' It was a morning for apologies. Mary came and apologised for getting drunk. Dad apologised to Dan for getting him lumbered with the washing up. I felt I should probably apologise simply for being alive. But Mum decided it was a good day for a family outing. 'There's a cheese museum I simply have to see. I mean, can you imagine what might be in it? It's in a nice town with a market and some good places to eat. I thought we could go and check out this silly museum, wander round the market, have lunch, go to the beach and then get back in plenty of time for the match. What do you say?'

'I suppose so,' said Dan unenthusiastically. Mum glared at him. 'Yes, great,' he said. 'Whatever.'

The idea of getting right away from the campsite did seem appealing. I didn't want to see Emma, or Mark, or Sonia, or Fergal or even Jacy very much today. I even felt like giving Becky a rest. 'OK. Let's go. Let's go now.'

'Can I get dressed first, please?' Dad stood there in his pyjamas looking dishevelled. His heroic drinking spree last night meant that he was rather the worse for wear. I went and sat in the car until they were all ready.

Mum drove and took charge of the day for all of us. It was a relief for me, and I suspect it was for Dan as well. We hadn't talked to each other properly for days.

The cheese museum was a hoot, all plastic cows

and cardboard cheeses, but it was in a beautiful sleepy town with a river running through it. The market was sleepy too, but there was a basket of incredibly cute puppies on sale. Dan is as soppy about that sort of thing as I am, and we played with them for as long as we dared. 'I'll have that one and I'll call him Dylan,' said Dan.

'And I'll have that one and I'll call him Dougal,' I said.

'Sure you don't mean Fergal?'

'Enough! No more teasing, OK?'

'Vous voulez acheter un petit chien?' An old crone was approaching us.

'Merci, non,' said Dan and we had to leave them behind.

'I thought we'd go somewhere where they serve seafood for lunch,' said Dad solemnly.

'Dad!'

He ducked. 'Only joking!'

'We're going to a crêperie,' said Mum. 'Perfect for fastidious teenage children. And I'm going to have some of their cider and sleep it off on the beach before driving home.' The parents were being particularly kind. Last night's little episode had reminded them that we were lucky to be a four-square family and they wanted to make the most of it. Danny and I went for a walk along the beach after lunch. There were rockpools and hidden coves to explore. At one point we were forced to scramble up to the top of the cliff and found ourselves walking down towards a naturists' beach.

'I think not,' I said.

'We could stay and look a while,' said Dan wistfully.

'There is a word for people like you, Daniel Morris!'

'OK! OK! I didn't mean it.'

'For someone who gets an eyeful of Suzette every day I'm surprised you feel the need.'

'All blokes feel the need, Sophie. Haven't you learnt that much?'

This was near-the-knuckle talk from Dan. 'What's the problem? Suzette's obviously crazy about you!'

'Do you think so?'

'DAN! You ask if *I* haven't learnt that much! Yes! I'm telling you, as a female, Suzette fancies the pants off you. And so does Emma. And that's the truth, I'm not being snidey.'

Dan went quite pink. 'Really? Both of them?' We slid down to the beach again. 'Gosh.'

'So are you going to do something about it?'

'Like what?'

'Oh Dan! Get off with one of them. I'd go for Suzette if I were you. She might teach you a thing or two.'

'But Emma—' his voice softened, 'Emma's more real somehow.'

'Up to you, brother dear. I don't fancy either of them as a sister-in-law, but that's not my problem.' Dan was quiet for a while after that. Fancy not realising, when both of them made it so obvious.

He gave me a bashful grin. 'Well, we'll just have to see what happens, won't we now?'

'Just don't leave it too long, or we'll have gone home and you'll have missed your chance.'

Mum and Dad were asleep on the beach. Dad had his arm across Mum's back. 'Aaah,' I said and quoted, 'Old people can be so sweet!' (I've watched *Clueless* nearly as many times as *Grease*.)

Back at the campsite it was football mania. There were signs everywhere as we drove up the hill.

FOOTBALL CE SOIR
ANGLETERRE V. FRANCE

Somebody had found some French flags and some Union Jacks and there were little kids running around with them. 'I feel sorry for the Dutch and the Germans,' said Dad as we pulled up.

'They're fine,' said Dan. 'They can be either French or English for the evening. No one takes it that seriously.'

'Strikes me that some of you are taking it very seriously indeed,' said Mum. 'All those practices.'

'We want to win', said Dan. 'Obviously. But since each side is such a mixture of nationalities, it's just our *team* that we want to win.'

'So no national pride allowed, then?' said Dad.

'No, none!' said Dan. 'Hey, Sophie, there's Becky!'

Becky was riding her bike in circles near the bar. She was wearing shorts and a top and a chiffon scarf round her neck. Dad tooted and she waved. She was waiting by our tent by the time I got out of the car. 'Come for a swim, Sophie,' she said. 'I want to hear all about the barbecue from hell! I asked Emma and Mark about it and Mark said it was great and Emma said it was ghastly and neither of them would say why.'

We went off to the pool. It was pleasantly empty. Most people were getting ready for the football in one way or another.

'Well?' she looked at me expectantly.

'Well. I had a row with my mum and my brother beforehand. And Emma and Mark's mum got horribly drunk. But the food was amazing. And – I sort of made my peace with Mark. We didn't say anything, I just felt I understood him a bit better.'

'Wow! Is this the Sophie Morris I know and love talking?'

'You don't have the monopoly on sympathy and niceness you know. Well, you do actually – but with your superb guidance I'm *learning*. See? I just felt sorry for the guy. No, not just sorry for him, that sounds patronising. I kind of felt I knew where he was coming from.'

'As I said, Wow.'

'Now, what about you and John?'

'We're cool.'

'I can't believe your dad hasn't noticed those lovebites on your neck.'

'I only take my scarf off to shower and swim, and since my dad doesn't accompany me on either occasion . . .'

'You mean he hasn't asked you why you're wearing a scarf in such hot weather?'

'I'll have you know this is a Gucci silk chiffon scarf.'

'Precisely!'

She splashed me. 'I've been spying on Sonia a bit. She and Jacy do seem to spend a lot of time together. She never seems to let him out of her sight!'

'Is she doing the football?'

'No. That's the only time she lets him go.'

'And then he's with *Emma*. I haven't told you this bit, have I? Jacy and Emma have been organising the football together. Jacy's the coach, Emma's the captain.'

'Oh! So that explains—'

'It does, except that Emma said—' I could hardly bring myself to tell even Becky about our exchange the night before.

'Go on,' said Becky.

'Well, it's part of what made last night so awful. Danny went and told Emma that I thought Jacy fancied me, and she said – she said, the cow, "I shouldn't think so," and then something incredibly condescending, like "Don't worry, I won't let on."' (As if every word of what she said wasn't imprinted on my brain.)

'So she thinks Jacy fancies *her*!' Becky's eyes widened and her mouth dropped open.

'I suppose she must do. What makes these girls think they're doing me a favour by warning me off?'

'It's obvious. They both think he's more interested in them. As if he could be, with you as competition. Don't worry, sweetie-pie, you'll get there in the end. I'm surprised at Emma though. I thought she had her heart set on your brother.'

'I think she probably has, but that wouldn't stop her thinking Jacy liked *her*, would it?'

'Hey-ho! what a complicated web we weave! We'd better get back. Supper's early for us – Gregory does not want to miss a nano-second of the footie. But then neither do John, Steve, Gus, Fergal – or anyone else for that matter.'

It was hard not to get caught up in the big match. It was a perfect evening like the first Monday night and about a hundred people gathered on the raised bank by the football pitch to sit on the grass and watch. Becky and I knew practically all the younger people in the teams. Danny, Mark, John, Steve and two of the Jamies were all playing for the English, along with Emma and Jacy, of course, and two sad girls we'd never spoken to. Fergal and Gus were playing for the French. So were Suzette and Monsieur from the Manoir and the Dutch dad from next door. Suzette in football gear had to be seen to be believed. My dad certainly had a look of disbelief on his face.

Jacy was a joy to watch, he was so graceful. So, to give her credit, was Emma. She darted about more like a dancer, fancy footwork was definitely her forte. But the star of the match was Fergal. Now I don't know much about football, but it was obvious even to me that he was a brilliant player. He was everywhere, always in the place where he was needed, his tall figure and his extraordinary coloured hair making him easy to follow. He seemed to have control of his whole team, even though he'd only just joined them. 'Ici! Ici!' and he'd be in the exact spot for them to get the ball to him easily so that he could score. At half-time it was two-one to the French. And very disgruntled the English team were, too.

The teams got into two huddles, a blue one (the French) and a white one (the English) to discuss their second-half tactics.

'Life won't be worth living in my family if the French win,' said Becky.

'Well Dan's very determined that it's only for fun,' I said. 'Have you any idea what's going to happen afterwards?'

'Party on the pitch I gather. The bar staff are setting up over there already. You know, it's true what the riding people were saying about Hélène. She never seems to get any time off.'

'I know. She was at the crêperie the night we arrived, the Acceuil most mornings and the bar every night since. I think the couriers only get one day off a week, too. Jacy was off last Tuesday. Of course, he was with Sonia then, in the evening. They were having a pizza together when I had my seafood fiasco.'

'But you don't really believe they're an item do you?'

'No. No more than I think he and Emma are. But I do get the feeling there's something else I should know.'

'Well, banish it from your mind instantly. I've got my heart set on getting you two together now. I've been here a week and I've never actually seen him even *touch* a girl other than you.'

'To date that includes fending me off when I bumped into him, seeing me back to my tent when I thought I was drunk, putting his hands over my eyes to say boo and bandaging my ankle. It's hardly what you'd call conclusive evidence.'

'Courage, dearheart! You forgot to mention *ruffling your hair*! And he bandaged your ankle very sexily. You told me so yourself.'

'Compared with what you and John obviously get up to, it's not a lot.'

'Me and John are different. Though he is getting a bit more romantic. He said today that he'd miss me when the holiday is over.'

'Oh, that's sweet.'

'I don't know if I'll miss him or not. I like his jokes. But you and Jacy were just meant to be. So hang on in there. Ooh. They're starting again.'

We lay on our fronts propped up on our elbows. I plucked at pieces of grass and found some juicy bits to chew. The light was beginning to fade as the match progressed. I drank in the sight of Jacy running, running, exhorting the others, punching the air, cheering. I could have watched him for ever and ever. I wanted them to win. I wanted to give him a triumphal hug.

But the French were doing well. Fergal scored two more goals. Each time, Suzette threw herself at him, true footballer fashion. Much ruffling of hair going on there. Even from this distance Fergal looked as if he was going to suffocate and die happy. Hmmm. Fergal and Suzette. How did I feel about that? Wasn't Suzette meant to like Dan? And wasn't Fergal meant to like me? No. Don't be greedy Sophie. It would solve Dan's problem. And it was Jacy I wanted, not Fergal. Fergal and Suzette was good. Really it was.

'Looks like Fergal's found himself an admirer,' commented Becky. 'Maybe he'll get over you. You'll both just have to pretend a little harder, won't you?' She sounded relieved.

'Uh-huh.' I supposed we would.

Jacy scored. Emma scored. Four-three to the French.

Fergal just missed a goal. Corner. To John. Who scored! Wow! Becky leapt to her feet. 'Wooohoooohooooweyhey! Yo JOHN!' Four-all. It was getting exciting. We were all on our feet.

Both teams were messing about. Only five minutes to go. Please don't let it be a draw. Suddenly Emma was weaving her way from one end of the pitch to the other. The ball was all hers. Mark was ready to take it. With sisterly intuition she slipped it to him. I saw Mark gather himself up and, would you believe it, another GOAL for the English! The crowd was going mad.

Two minutes to go and there was Fergal, determined to be there to the end. He motioned Suzette into place and readied himself to pass the ball to her. The English were so sure of victory they hardly noticed. The goalie was looking the other way. Suzette was concentrating. Fergal gave her the ball. She swung her leg back – and then – she buckled! She missed the ball completely, landing on the ground at the same time as the whistle went. Oh dear! How *humiliating* for her.

The English had won. But only just. If only Fergal had taken the shot himself. But he'd wanted to give Suzette, who really was French, a chance.

'What a guy,' said Becky with a sigh. 'The rest of the team will be furious with him, except they won't dare, because it was all down to him anyway. And it was a good result. Our team would have been gutted if they'd lost after all their practice. Now, excuse me while I go and hug my man.' It's amazing what a goal does to a girl.

It was a brilliant night. *Everyone* was hugging and kissing each other! I tolerated a sweaty bear hug from Mark and an even sweatier one from Jacy. But then so did all the other girls in the vicinity. Somehow it didn't matter. The good humour was palpable. It was an excellent day for international relations.

It was definitely a family occasion. Having the grown-ups and little kids around made it less fun in some ways, but more relaxed in others. People were so nice to each other. Even Emma, though she was high as a kite on her success, came over to me and said she was sorry she upset me the other night and I said I was sorry I had mouthed off at her and what a brilliant match etc. etc. Fergal was hugged to death by every one, male and female, as he made his way over to our group. 'Well played, man!' he said to Emma, who took it as a compliment. He sat down next to me, near Gus and Steve and John and Becky. 'Did you enjoy the match then?'

'Impossible not to,' I said, trying to see where Jacy was. He was over by the bar hitting the beer.

Fergal lay back on the bank. 'I'm completely knackered. I'm out of training.'

'Me too,' said all the other boys in unison.

'I'm not going to last out much longer,' said John apologetically to Becky.

'That's OK,' said Becky. 'I think you're all heroes – and heroines,' she said as Danny and Mark came over with Emma and Suzette.

'Hi guys,' said Dan as they sat down.

'Ooh, *interesting*,' said Becky to me under her breath. 'Suzette coming over to see Fergal.'

'More interesting than you think,' I whispered. 'Danny's only just found out that both Emma and Suzette fancy him – if she still does now, of course – and he doesn't know which one to go for!'

'It has to be Emma. Doesn't it?' Becky whispered back.

But Emma was turning to go away again. 'I just want to catch Jacy before he gets completely out of it,' she said.

'I thought couriers didn't get drunk on duty,' I said.

'They don't. But he's off duty until Wednesday now, so I expect he's about to make the most of it!'

'Shower for me and bed, I reckon,' said Dan.

'Me too,' said Mark.

'Et tu, Suzette?' said Dan. 'Es tu fatiguée?'

Suzette smiled wickedly. 'Oui, but I like to shower too!' she said. All five boys keeled over.

Danny looked over at me. 'OK, Suzette,' he said. 'I'll escort you to the shower block.

'Me too,' said Gus and Steve.

'They're mad,' said Fergal.

'I agree,' said John. 'Come on Becky. How about you escorting me to the shower block?'

'OK,' said Becky.

Fergal stood up. 'See you tomorrow, Sophie,' he said. 'I'll escort you, Mark, if you'll escort me.'

'You'll be OK?' said Mark to me as I sat there on my own. And then, 'Here comes Emma. You two can go back together.'

And there was me, raring to go. What a let down. Jacy on a bender and everyone else too tired even to talk. And what did I get? I got Emma. Still, it had been fun. Emma came up. 'Where've all the others gone? I couldn't get any sense out of Jacy so I gave up.'

'Off to have showers.'

'Yeah, I could do with one myself. I'm finished.'

'You were very good,' I said.

'Thanks. We do girls' football at school. We often beat the boys. I'm going to be captain next term.' She looked at me with pride. 'Even though I'm the youngest.'

'I'm impressed,' I said. It wasn't altogether a lie. I had been impressed by her playing. We walked past the crêperie and the bar together and stood briefly in the light before plunging down the dark path that led to our tents.

'Er – did Dan go off with Suzette just now?' She looked at me anxiously. Ha! the POWER. But I suddenly saw in that troubled look some of the shadows that had crossed Mark's eyes the night before.

'Him and ten million others. Anyway Suzette seems to have the hots for Fergal, now, didn't you notice?'

'No,' she said. 'Can't say I did.' We'd reached our tents. Her mum was there, asleep on a sunbed in the dark, an empty wine bottle by her side. She'd missed the match.

'Emma,' I said.

'Yes?'

'My brother likes you, you know.'

She stopped in her tracks. 'Really?'

'Yup. Have a nice shower! Goodnight.'

Twelve

Apart from the tedious man two tents away who called his office every day on the dot of nine on his mobile, giving useless instructions to people who were clearly getting on fine without him, all was quiet long into the morning. Even the little Dutch kids filed off to the shower block later than usual. I lay dozing, remembering bits about last night and smiling to myself. Dan had come back with Mark, not long after me. They had whispered together for a while, but Dan had fallen straight into bed and I'd not had the energy to get up and talk to him.

I thought it was time I updated my diary. I hauled it out of my bag. If Jacy wasn't going to be around today in person I could spend time with him on paper. A lot had happened since I last wrote, so I tried to remember a bit about each day. Then I looked back at what I'd written about Jacy and Mark before. My feelings about Jacy hadn't altered, though my opinion of Mark had undergone a U-turn.

Jacy

Jacy is as gorgeous as ever. The sight of him playing football last night will last me for a long time, not to mention a sweaty clinch with him after the match. He's very strong. Strong hands too. He even has nice-smelling sweat. Sonia seems to want him for herself, and I thought Emma did too. They both warned me off him for no good reason. I'm getting desperate – might have to resort to desperate measures. I just know he'll be wonderful. I'm still worried about being too young for him. Perhaps I'll have to let him know that I love him so much I'm prepared to go further with him. I think I would – for him. I mean, it's all right, if you love someone, isn't it? I can't believe I'm so confused. It must be the real thing! I hope no one reads this.

Mark

I could still never fancy him in a million years, but I don't think he's awful any more. I don't even mind Emma so much. Their dad has left them and their mum has a drink problem, though she's nice otherwise. For the record, he does have a personality and a sense of humour, and even his blue eyes have a certain appeal.

Fergal

I ought to put in a bit about Fergal because he's helping me to get Jacy. I've never met anyone remotely like Fergal before. He has dark red curls and his eyes have clear blue irises without any darker lines round them like Ms O'Reirdan at school. He's tall but not too skinny and good at fooball and dancing. Oh yes, and he has a terrific voice. Suzette seems to fancy him, so he'll be the envy of most of the boys. He's nice too, and quite deep, and now I'm used to it I like his Irish accent.

115

I did a little list of couples and potential couples:

Becky	*John*
Emma	*Dan*
Suzette	*Fergal*
Me	*Jacy*

with lots of question marks and hearts around it. That was enough. Time to get up.

'So what was it like having a shower with Suzette?' I asked Danny over breakfast. Dad looked up sharply from his *Sud-Ouest* newspaper.

'Pardon me? You had a shower with Suzette?'

'Hardly likely, Dad. They have male and female shower blocks in case you hadn't noticed. But we did shout over the walls quite a bit, yes. And we did throw Fergal's shorts over to her and she threw her top over to us. Which left Fergal in his underpants and her in her bra. But we're broadminded. It's not as if we don't spend most of the day wearing less.'

'Well, I really don't know what young people are coming to these days,' said Dad.

'Hypocrite!' said Dan goodnaturedly. 'And you a teenager in the sixties and seventies. You all had love-ins in the nude didn't you?'

'Sadly, no,' said Dad. 'Not in Welwyn Garden City anyway.'

'Anyway,' said Dan to me, 'That's what happened in the showers. We all thought Fergal and Suzette needed a little encouragement.'

'And did it work?'

'Suzette was keen, but Fergal wouldn't go for it.'

'Strange lad,' said Dad, behind his newspaper again.

'Well, she is a bit of a bimbo.'

'Oy, sexist!' Mum chimed in. 'Just because she's stunning.'

'She's stunning, but she's stupid.'

'Oh well,' said Mum. 'I suppose I should be glad that a son of mine heeds brains over beauty.'

I was relieved about that. I was dreading Dan making a major play for Suzette after what I'd said to Emma.

It was a strange, hazy day. Sea mists, Mum said. It felt like the aftermath of something. Dan was thoughtful. Emma and Mark next door were having subdued conversations with their mum. Becky didn't appear as she usually did. We couldn't even hear Gus singing or shouting his way round the campsite as on other days. There was a tennis tournament in the afternoon. Emma was playing, but no one else we knew.

After lunch I biked over to Becky's. Her mum told me that she was with John and Steve. I found her there. She and John were in the caravilla making coffee in apparent domestic bliss. Steve leapt up as soon as I came in. 'Sophie! Rescue me from these lovebirds! Tell me you'll come swimming.'

'Hi!' said Becky. 'I don't want to come swimming because I've got my period.'

John wore a self-consciously grown-up expression as she imparted this news but Steve said, 'You didn't have to share that with us, you know.'

'Why on earth not?' said Becky. 'You might as well know that I'm not just being boring. What's the point in pretending I've got better things to do?'

Steve cowered. 'All right. Sorry. But you're OK – to swim – are you Sophie?'

'That's why I'm here. The campsite's dead today. Where are the Irish lads?'

'We'll go and see, shall we?' said Steve.

The Irish encampment was almost down by the lake. I

hadn't been there before. They had one big tent and three little pup tents. Gus was still sleeping, apparently – at two o'clock in the afternoon. Peter and Sean were seated companionably round a table with their parents, listening to cricket on the radio. Fergal was sitting cross-legged in the entrance of his tent, writing.

'Say you've come to offer to fetch ice-creams for us!' said Sean.

'Sean!' his mum reprimanded him. 'You're so lazy!'

'But I don't want to miss the match!'

'I didn't know it was on,' said Steve. 'Can I stay and listen with you?'

'I'll get ice-creams,' I said. 'I've nothing better to do. Though I haven't got any money.'

Their dad said, 'I'm ashamed of you all, but if you're offering, sweetheart, I'll pay for yours, to be sure.' I took their orders and their money.

'Mango for me,' said Fergal. 'And I'd love to come with you, but I'm wanting to finish this while it's in me head.'

'I'll help you,' said Peter. 'You might not manage to carry eight and I've lost interest in the match.'

Peter and I set off walking together to the bar. 'What was Fergal writing?' I asked him.

'Who knows?' said Peter. 'Fergal's always writing things. Has done as long as I've known him. Might be a poem' (he pronounced it poyim) 'or a song or a letter or anything really. Might be a fairy-story. You never can tell with me old pal Fergal Maguire.'

'Quite a talented bloke, Fergal, isn't he?' I said.

'And that's an understatement! I've lived in his shadow most of me life. I ought to be envious of the guy, but you see he's not competitive like that. It's just the way he is. And he's always had this air of tragedy surrounding him, you know, because of his mother dying and all, so he can be good at things and people don't hate him for it. Quite the opposite. The girls love him.'

'I haven't noticed him taking advantage of all this adulation.'

'Well, no. He's picky. Bit of a romantic. Still believes in love and all that.'

'You sound very cynical.'

'Me? No. Just practical. I just fancy Julia Roberts and Marilyn Monroe, Suzette and Sophie, and know they wouldn't look twice at me even if they could. So I'll take what I can when it comes my way. High expectations in love make people very unhappy, don't you think?'

'I'll think about that one, Peter. Now are you going to ask Hélène in French or am I? Or shall we just point?'

We went into the sudden darkness of the bar. There was a harassed dad with a crowd of tinies round the ice-cream cabinet. He struggled to get his order out in French and the girl serving him said, 'So, zat is two vanillas, two strawberries, one blackcurrant and mango and one chocolate and pistache. Zat will be sirty francs please.' It wasn't Hélène. I couldn't imagine Hélène saying all that in English.

I gave the new girl our order and asked 'Where's Helene today? Has she finally got the day off to see her boyfriend?' It was nosy I know, but the place seemed strangely empty without Hélène smouldering behind the bar. I didn't like to think of her as Cinderella, all work and no play.

She looked up from her task of pressing perfect boules of ice-cream into cones. 'Oh yes, Hélène is wiz her boyfriend today, so I work! Here we are. Zat will be forty francs, s'il vous plait.'

Cut to happy boys eating dripping ices. Cut again to the pool, a late and lazy afternoon, people drifting to join us, including Emma, who had not done well at tennis, and Danny commiserating and attentive. Including Suzette who, in the face of Fergal's lack of enthusiasm had, to her surprise – and his – unleashed a superabundance of it on Steve. Cut right past the huddle in the bar without Hélène, or Jacy for that matter, and to the bonfire. A mellow bonfire, built and tended by Mark. It seems as if we've done this every night of our lives. We're sitting round the fire, John and Becky, Steve and Suzette, Dan and Emma, me, Fergal and a guitar. The others are here too: Francine, Gus, Sean and Peter, the Jamies, the Kates, Tristan. We're all singing kiddie songs, like 'Yellow Submarine' and 'Nellie the Elephant'. The sky clears for the first time today and we lie on our backs gazing at the enormity of the universe laid out up there. The fire burbles and hisses whenever Mark chucks on another piece of wood. The moon, big and benign, rises slowly.

'There's the Plough,' said Steve, to impress Suzette.

'Everyone can see the Plough,' said Tristan, the Brain, 'but can you make out the three stars of Orion's belt? Follow them and you come to the Pole star. And that swathe of white stuff is the Milky Way – our galaxy, and over there, that bright reddish one, that's Betelguese –'

'Eh, you've lost me, mate. Beetlejuice?' said Steve, making Suzette giggle. She had even more trouble understanding him than I did.

Fergal rolled onto his side to face me. 'The stars in the sky are the eyes of the angels looking down upon our souls making sure we've done not'ing wrong.'

'What's that?'

'It's what my grandma told me when I was young. I used to think that my mum was up there.'

'Why shouldn't she be there?'

'Because, as Tristan says, we know what is there.'

'I prefer not to know everything like that. After all, no

one's been there. They don't really know! I want to keep stars romantic.'

'But don't you love the way the stars make our lives seem so small and insignificant? If each one of those is a sun and maybe each one has its own planets and on each of those there are millions of life forms? We're just specks! Tiny specks that mean nothing!'

'I think that's scary. I don't want to be a tiny speck that means nothing.'

'Not now, not when you're happy, but when you're sad and the whole world seems a terrible miserable place, then it's good to know that we're no more than grains of sand.'

'You don't feel that right now do you?'

He turned onto his back, with his knees bent and his hands behind his head. 'No,' he said, 'Right now I'm very content.'

'Me too, for the moment.' It had been a peaceful day without Jacy. I still looked for him everywhere and saw him everywhere, turning my face to his sun. I longed for that moment when we finally stopped running and he held me in his arms. I wished I was lying here with him instead of Fergal. The irony of lying by the glowing embers – not with him! Or looking at the stars – not with him! It almost made me want to weep. Tomorrow night, that would be my moment. At the disco – I was going to tell him how I felt. I wouldn't leave anything to chance this time.

Mark appeared with an armful of wood. 'It's getting chilly. It's getting chilly.' He threw it on the fire, making sparks fly up into the air.

'My back was getting damp,' said Becky.

'Ho-ho,' said Steve. 'I wish Suzette's was.'

Becky ignored him. John put his arm round her protectively and drew her towards him as they sat by the fire. 'More music, Fergal!' said Danny. I saw that he and Emma were sitting very close to one another, too. Emma was wearing his sweatshirt.

'It is getting nippy, isn't it?' I said to Fergal.

'Have my jacket,' he said, shrugging it off. 'It gets in the way when I play.' I put it on. It smelt of woodsmoke.

This wasn't a singsong any more. It was Fergal playing and singing alone. People were sitting with their arms round one another for warmth, in groups and pairs even if they weren't couples. Fergal said I could lean against him so I sat warming my back against his, his movements transmitted through my body as he played. It was very soothing. He had a nice back. I could feel his spine and the muscles across his shoulders. I could feel the vibrations of his voice on the low notes, and sometimes his hair on my neck where mine had parted. It was kind of sexy. I pretended he was Jacy.

'Anyone else want a turn?' Fergal held up his guitar.

'I will,' said Gus. 'Prove that Fergal Maguire is not the only Irishman round here who can sing. Give us your guitar, Fergal.' Fergal handed the guitar over to Gus, but quickly put out his other arm to stop me falling as he upset our perfectly balanced back-to-back arrangement. Gus started strumming. Mark fed the fire, and a hard core – about a dozen – of us lingered on.

I saw John and Becky, their soft, lovers' faces lit up by the firelight, Dan and Emma, serious – Dan had a tentative arm around her, Steve and Suzette, giggling. Steve barely believing his good fortune. Tristan had got together with one of the Kates and one of the Jamies was with the other one. Francine and some Dutch girls were cuddled up with Sean and Peter.

And there was me, with Fergal. We sat facing forwards, his jacket round both of us. I had my arms round my knees but he had his arm round my shoulders, ostensibly to keep me warm. I couldn't pretend that he wasn't fiddling with my hair, and I don't think it was to keep his hand warm. Apart from that we kept perfectly still, breathing in unison. It felt very private. No one else could possibly notice.

The fire was going down. Mark was singing along quietly with Gus. Fergal's fingers in my hair gently touched my ear. It was the most imperceptible of moves, but it was a move all the same. I looked at him questioningly.

He was gazing at me with those depthless blue eyes. 'You're very, very beautiful,' he said. 'Did you know, your hair shines out, even when it's dark? It's as though it's lit up with a thousand little fires and stars.'

'Fergal—' I began, but he leant forward and kissed my lips, once, just gently.

'I'm sorry,' he said, drawing back. 'I got carried away – ever so slightly. I hope you don't mind.'

I felt confused. For over a week I had wanted nothing more than to be kissed by Jacy. Imagined it. Felt it. But the kiss had come from Fergal. Fergal Maguire, who I had been sitting close to all evening, breathing with him, moving with him, feeling his warmth, the tickle of his hair, the smell of his clothes. Was this the moment to tell him that I felt nothing at all for him, everything for someone else? Was it even true?

The party was breaking up. Torchlight flashed across the field as people made their way back to their tents. 'Here's your guitar, Fergal,' said Mark, as we stood up.

'Go for it, Fergal,' said Gus loudly, punching him on the shoulder and walking on. We stood by the embers, the last to leave, no torch. I shivered.

'It's going to be very dark in the woods. I'll walk you back, Sophie,' said Fergal.

'Thank you,' I said, and slipped my arm round his waist. I don't know quite what I meant by the gesture. I wanted to let him know that I did like him, even though he already knew from Becky that I was in love with Jacy.

We made our way through the trees, stumbling and giggling a little, but we didn't speak. I kept my arm round his waist, feeling the sinewy strength of his tall frame as we walked.

As we came to our tent I spotted Dan giving Emma a peck on the cheek, but judging by the way they gazed longingly at each other before letting go their hands and going their separate ways, some understanding had been reached. My, how romance was in the air!

Fergal whispered, 'I'd like to kiss you again.'

I looked up at him and said, 'Well, yes, as long as you understand—' but I couldn't finish my sentence because he was kissing me and clasping me very tightly.

'It's my last day tomorrow,' he said, letting go of me, but holding both my hands in his. 'You're very lovely, Sophie. I don't expect you to fall for a fellow like me – but maybe, tomorrow night, you'll save me the last dance?' And he was off into the night before I could answer, or finish that sentence – 'as long as you understand that I'm in love with someone else.' It seemed that he'd never even been told.

Thirteen

'I've got a bone to pick with you.'

Becky waved goodbye to John before turning to me. 'Come again?'

'Becky, you never told Fergal anything, did you?'

She gave me a wobbly smile. 'What do you mean?'

'You were supposed to ask Fergal to pretend to fancy me so we could make Jacy jealous.'

'Well, he already did. Obviously still does! Nudge, nudge, wink, wink! Go on, Sophie, tell me what happened. Let's ride over to the horses, something to do.'

'Oh, OK.' I got on my bike and we cycled off together. But I wasn't letting her off the hook. 'Now listen. We agreed that you would tell Fergal that I was in love with Jacy and that we needed his help. I tried to get you to tell me precisely what you'd said to him, but you changed the subject, I seem to remember.'

'Lighten up, Sophie. You and Fergal were obviously getting along very well together last night. What's the problem?'

'The problem is that I assumed he knew there was someone else. And that we were just friends.'

'Is that how you behave with friends? I can't imagine you letting me kiss you as we snuggled up together by the fire!'

'Becky, don't be disgusting! Anyway, I didn't think anybody saw that.'

'I'm your friend. I saw it.'

'Well, as I said. I thought he knew it didn't mean anything, because of my feelings for Jacy, but it all got embarrassing when I realised he didn't know. And that's your fault.'

'All right, so I didn't actually mention Jacy. I didn't think I'd need to. It suddenly seemed a juvenile thing to ask Fergal to do. He's quite an awesome guy. And he obviously fancied you anyway.'

'Do you mean you didn't say *any*thing?'

'Well, I said something, but not in so many words,' she muttered.

'BECKY!' I bellowed. 'Once and for all tell me what you

said and didn't say, so I know where I stand. I don't believe this!'

Becky looked a little shamefaced. 'OK. Now don't shout at me, because you're not going to like this.'

'GO ON!'

'I said, don't shout. I went to Fergal all prepared to say what we'd agreed. I went to him, and at that very moment he was looking in your direction – all longingly. I was going to ask him to pretend to like you, but I saw that it wouldn't be necessary. And he's a cool guy, Fergal – like I said, it suddenly seemed very much the wrong thing to do at that precise moment. So then I thought, if he liked you anyway, there needn't be any pretending involved, so it would be much more realistic. So—' she faltered. 'So I didn't – er – say anything.'

'You didn't say anything at all?'

'Er – no. I lied.'

I stopped and got off my bike. 'HOW COULD YOU!' I screamed. 'So all the time Fergal must have thought I was going after him. Oh my God.'

Becky had stopped too. 'Well, I kind of thought that maybe you'd suit each other.'

'So – the other plan – have you been lying about that all along? All that "you and Jacy were meant for each other" stuff – were you just making it up? Just to please me? String me along? Poor little Sophie. Me and my ugly boyfriend are OK thank you very much but let's play at fantasy romance for her!'

Becky spoke very quietly. 'You shouldn't have said that, Sophie.'

I was too wound up to speak, though I knew I'd overstepped the mark.

She still spoke quietly, almost menacingly. 'I got cold feet. It didn't seem fair to "use" Fergal. But you don't seem to mind "using" people, do you?'

I knew I had to apologise. 'Becky!' She was getting on her bike again. 'Becky! I'm sorry!'

'Huh! Never thought I'd hear you say that!'

'Becky! Please!' Suddenly the tears welled up and I was crying. 'I'm sorry. I didn't mean to say anything so horrible. John isn't ugly. You know he isn't. I'm just – *jealous!*' And that was the truth. John and Becky had a lovely thing going. They were both lovely people. They had each other and I had no one.

'I just feel bad about leading Fergal on. It seemed all right if he knew. But now he's going to think—' I was crying again.

Becky, big, kind Becky, threw her bike down and put her arms round me. 'It's OK. I'm sorry I didn't level with you and I know you didn't mean it about John. Fergal's not stupid. Did he even try to find out if you had anyone else?'

'No. And I didn't ask him. We only kissed once – well twice.'

'That's nothing! What are you worrying about? Tell you what. Let's spend today getting you ready for the disco. You look gorgeous anyway, but let's make you totally irresistible. I'll give you a makeover and do your hair and nails and stuff. And you can borrow some of my clothes if you like.'

I sniffed. 'Where's John gone today?'

'Their parents have taken them off in search of culture. Much against Steve's wishes. He's just discovered culture here! But they'll be back in time for the disco. And it's the Irish guys' last night, isn't it? So we won't have to worry about Fergal after tomorrow anyway. Now cheer up. Operation Seduction is under way. Jacy will not know what has hit him! But let's say hello to the horses first.'

I was going to miss Becky when this holiday was over. 'Becky?'

'Are you going to shout at me or insult my boyfriend this time?'

'Becky, let's write to each other when we get home.'

'Won't you be too busy writing to Jacy at medical school?'

We called in at our tent. I grabbed a peach for lunch and told Mum where I was going.

'Eat more than that, darling!'

'Stop fussing, Mum.' I didn't feel the slightest bit hungry.

'She'll have supper with us later,' said Becky.

'I don't suppose you'll starve then,' said Mum. 'Drop by on your way to the disco, both of you. I want to see what you look like.'

'We'll look a million dollars!' said Becky. With Becky's wardrobe that probably wasn't far off the truth, but I wanted something tight-fitting as well, so I grabbed my white dress. Mum had just washed it. It was dazzlingly clean and sweetsmelling from drying in the sun and nice and clingy. And I was a lot browner than when I'd last worn it.

We cycled over to Becky's. I felt all fluttery and excited. Tonight was the night! I didn't want Jacy to see me until I was all dressed up. 'Try on clothes first,' said Becky, 'Because that's what takes the longest. Then legs and armpits. Then you can have a face mask and maybe I'll give you a manicure. Then a shower, and I'll pluck your eyebrows while your hair's drying off. Then dress, then hair, nail varnish and make-up.' And we only had six hours.

'What am I going to s—'

'Don't talk!' said Becky, buffing my nails. 'You'll spoil the face mask!' I turned towards her. 'Don't move or those cucumber slices will fall off.'

I wanted to talk to Becky about what I should say to Jacy so that he was in no doubt about how I felt. I'd tried asking her before, but her line was that I was going to look so devastating that words would be unnecessary. One look and he'd be bewitched. I didn't want her advice exactly, just reassurance. I now had smooth-as-silk arm-pits and legs and my outfit for the evening hung over the chair in Becky's tiny room in the caravilla. I lay on her bed, my face plastered in goo with cucumber slices on my eyes while Becky filed my bitten nails into shape, ready for several coats of gold glittery nail varnish.

I was going to wear my white dress with one of her filmy blouses. It was made of a beautiful opalescent material like a dragonfly's wings. She wouldn't let me wear my trainers with the white dress as I normally did, but persuaded me to borrow a pair of her strappy high-heeled sandals. She also lent me a simple pale gold chain for my neck because she said it was the same colour as my hair.

'Five more minutes,' said Becky, 'and then you can talk. I'll go and get some drinks from the fridge for when you can move again.'

I took the cucumber slices off my eyes and sat up. 'Now go and wash that stuff off,' said Becky. 'There are loads of cotton wool balls by the basin.' Great. My face felt tingly and fresh, but that was probably because it wasn't covered in stuff any more. 'Lovely!' said Becky when I came back, though I couldn't see any difference myself. 'Have a drink and then you'd better get in the shower and wash your hair. It's already half-past four. Only three-and-a-half hours to go!'

'What do you think I—'

'We'll talk while I'm doing your nail varnish. Get in the shower and wash your hair now. There should be some conditioner in there too. Take your time. I'm

129

going to sort out what I'm going to wear while you're in there.'

It was a cramped little shower in the caravilla, but at least the water was hot. Becky and her mum had a whole range of wonderful designer shower gels, body lotions, shampoos, conditioners. Not like the Boots stuff my mum buys. It was a real treat. I wrapped a towel round me and another one round my hair and went obediently to have my nails varnished while my hair dried off.

'What do you think of this outfit? Ta-da!' Becky did a twirl. She was wearing a beautifully cut black blouse with a deep neck that showed off her cleavage and the gorgeous Moschino jeans that she'd been wearing the first time I saw her. She held her hair up in a topknot.

'Becky, you look lovely! Black really suits you and you look good with your hair scraped back like that.'

'No need to go over the top.'

'No, I mean it.'

'I suppose black does have a slimming effect.'

'Shut up. John will be bowled over. Let me do your nails when you've done mine, and I'll have a go at your hair for you too.'

Becky changed back into her shorts and top. 'Isn't this great? I wouldn't mind if we never even went to the disco. Getting ready is by far the best bit.'

'It is usually, but tonight is pretty important for me. You've got to help me, Becky! Do I just go up to him and say, "Take me I'm yours"? What if I can't even get him to dance with me? What if he's all over Sonia?'

'What you want is a sort of "my place or yours?" line. 'Or "I hope you're feeling as hot as I am tonight"'

'Except that he'll just offer to open a window!'

'How about simply, "I want to make *lurve* to you, baby. We can go to my place if you like".'

'Because my place is a tiny compartment in a tent and my parents will be there.'

'Well, you know what I mean.'

'I think I'm just going to have to persuade him to dance with me first and hope it's a slow one. And then act all – seductive. You know, press up against him, nibble his earlobe sort of thing.'

'You'll have to go up to him and ask him to dance in a way that he can't refuse. Very straight, even – "I want to thank you for being a marvellous courier, so please dance this one with me—"'

'Oh yeah! Irresistible!' We both fell about laughing.

' "Young man! Let me clasp you to my bosom as a way of showing my appreciation of your superb ability as a courier!" Now keep your hand still or you'll muck this nail varnish up.'

It was a problem though. I'd never felt so unsure of myself. Such a big step, going from little meetings here and there to the in-your-face 'how about getting off with me?' question. Fine if he came on to me, but I wasn't sure I could pull it off if I had to do the asking. I'd never had to do it that way round before.

'It's gone six o'clock!'

'Aagh. I feel all nervous and clammy. I still don't feel like eating.'

'But we'd better eat before we dress up. Come on. I can smell cooking already. Here, put my dressing gown on.' Needless to say, I didn't eat a thing.

We teetered out at ten to eight. We both wore more make-up than usual and we'd put our hair up. Becky had done a really good job on mine. We had to walk rather than cycle, and even that was difficult with high heels. I'm not used to them, especially with a dodgy ankle. Mark and Emma were coming back with their washing-up as we got to our tent. Mark whistled. And then blushed.

'Is everyone dressing up for the disco, then?' asked Emma, taking us in.

'We're not *that* dressed up!' I said.

'We only spent the entire afternoon getting ready,' said Becky. 'But that was because we had fun doing it,' she added, catching my eye.

'I'd better change then,' said Emma. 'But I didn't bring anything glamorous.'

'I've got another dress like this, in pale blue,' I said. 'You can borrow it if you like. It would suit you.'

Emma flushed with pleasure. 'Could I really? I'd look after it.'

' 'Course. I'll get it.'

'Wow!' said my dad when he saw us. 'You two look stunning. I hope the young fellows appreciate it.'

I got out the blue dress and took it to Emma. Danny was sitting at their table. 'That will look pretty on you,' he said as Emma disappeared into the tent to put it on.

'Bless him,' said Becky. 'Come on Sophie. Let's hit the bar first.'

It was still the other girl behind the bar. Becky and I drank Bleu Tropiques and waited for the boys. I was more nervous than I would have imagined possible. My thoughts had been so focused on Jacy all afternoon that I'd put Fergal and last night to the back of my mind. I wasn't prepared for my feelings when he came in. He was wearing a white T-shirt and jeans, nothing special, but I'd only ever seen him in baggy things and football gear before, so I was surprised at how fit he looked.

'Girls! Beer!' shouted Gus.

'Can I sit here?' Fergal asked tentatively.

I wasn't sure whether to say 'yes' and be accused of

leading him on again, but I was saved by John saying, 'Sorry mate, but this bit of glamour is mine,' as he slid in beside Becky. Then Steve sat next to John and Suzette sat next to Steve, so Fergal was stranded at the opposite end of the table from me. But Fergal wasn't really my concern.

When we all finally moved in a great crowd to the disco he caught up with me. 'Sophie, you look divine. Truly, like a goddess, all white and gold.' He looked me over. 'Even your skin is golden.' There was no answer to that. 'I've got a little poem for you. Save that last dance for me and you shall have it. And then I'll be bothering you no more. We'll be gone like the dew before you even open your beautiful eyes in the morning.' And he strode on because Peter was calling him.

Jacy was the first person I saw when we arrived at the crêperie, where the disco was being held. He wore a yellow shirt, so I couldn't miss him. He smiled and waved as we made our entrance. My stomach lurched. How was I going to carry this off? I just wanted him too badly.

I sat down to psych myself up and watched. There was plenty to look at. Our group swirled in and out of my vision. Danny and Emma. He was right – she did look pretty in the pale blue dress, and her face was lit up with happiness. John and Becky. He was still mesmerised by the black blouse. Steve and Suzette. Mark, Fergal. The couriers were all there. It had the feeling of a grand finale. I just HAD to do it.

I stood up. Jacy was across the floor from me. He had been dancing with Sonia but now she was talking to Coralie and he was on his own. I steadied myself and started to walk towards him. But damn. Fergal was right beside me. Fergal was intercepting me. I couldn't be doing with this, I'd lose my nerve.

'Sophie?'

'Not now, Fergal! Go away! Leave me alone! I have to talk to Jacy!' He looked puzzled. 'You don't understand! I'm in love with Jacy. I don't want you! Please!'

I was incoherent but Fergal got the message. 'I'm sorry,' he said, backing away. 'I didn't realise.' He looked at me, crushed, his eyes misty. I couldn't bear it. 'But—' He looked towards Jacy. 'Never mind, I'll go. I'll be away.'

I had to keep going. I went up to Jacy. My legs weren't working and those few steps seemed like a million miles.

'Hi Sophie!' he said, cheerily, as if everything was normal.

I went right up to him, as close as I dared. I looked deep into his eyes. 'I am a sunflower,' I breathed, hotly.

'I beg your pardon?'

'I mean—' Oh God, he was smiling down at me, all shining eyes and sexy mouth. 'Dance me.'

The next record was a fast one but I wasn't going to be put off my stride now, oh no. I put my arms round Jacy's neck and moved my hips slowly from side to side, despite the fact that he was jigging about. I wished he'd keep still. I put my mouth to his ear. 'Jacy,' I whispered, 'I'm completely crazy.' He was trying to pull away. I didn't want him to pull away. I kept my arms locked about his neck.

'Sophie, are you all right?' My legs had turned to water. I knew I was losing it but I had to soldier on. It was my last chance.

'Kiss it to me,' I groaned, and fainted clean away.

When I came to, Jacy was crouching beside me, flapping a bit of paper as a fan. There was quite a crowd. Groggily I sat up and looked around at the circle of faces peering down. And then it happened. Suddenly, from being a blur, everything slid into focus. Hélène appeared from nowhere. She broke through the circle and knelt beside Jacy. She looked at me and she looked at him. 'Jean-Claude? Qu'est ce que ce passe, chéri?' she asked.

'C'est la jeune Sophie,' he said. He spoke French like a native because he *was* a native. 'La pauvre enfant.'

'The French courier,' I croaked, and passed out again.

Fourteen

I thought Jacy would have run a mile, but he didn't. He knelt down beside me and propped me up against him while Hélène got me a drink of water. Then together they walked me outside and sat me on a bench to get some fresh air. They talked to each other in French the whole time. Then Jacy asked gently, 'Would you like someone to be with you?'

'Becky,' I said. So Jacy left me with Hélène and went off to find Becky. I felt embarrassed to be with Hélène, but at least she hadn't come on the scene until after I fainted, so she hadn't seen me trying to get off with Jacy. I'm sure he'd told her something in French, but she wasn't holding it against me. Quite the reverse. She was incredibly kind, stroking my hair and offering me sips of water.

Jacy came back. But Becky wasn't with him. Mark was. 'I couldn't find Becky, but Mark offered to come and take you back to your tent. Will you be all right now?'

I couldn't look at Jacy. 'Yes. Thank you,' I said, feeling dreadful.

'Sophie?' Jacy crouched down beside me again, forcing me to look at him. 'There have obviously been some misunderstandings. I'm sorry. I'll come and see you tomorrow – OK?' I gave him a watery smile. 'That's better.' He stood up and gave Mark a friendly punch on the shoulder. 'Cheers mate!' Spoken like a true Frenchman.

'Where did Becky get to?' I asked Mark.

'She and John weren't around. I saw what happened, Sophie, but I don't think anyone else did. Don't worry.'

Three sentences, all of them different. Was this a record? I was about to say something about him being able to jeer at me now, but I could see that he wasn't jeering.

'I tried a warn ya, Sophie.'

'Don't remind me, Mark. I was so rude to you then I'm surprised you're still speaking to me.'

'You've got a temper on you, I know. I've dealt with worse.'

'Can we go somewhere else, Mark? I don't want to see anyone. I was unspeakable to Fergal back there, too. So I've blown it with just about everybody really.'

'We could go and find Fergal.'

'No, I don't think so . . .'

'We c'n go and sit in a field near the horses if ya want.'

'Thanks. I don't want to go back to my tent or down to the lake. I'll just have to write to the Irish boys.'

'I've got their addresses.'

We walked towards the stables. We could hear the horses chomping and rustling. We found some straw bales to sit on in the field.

'This is really nice of you, Mark.'

'It's OK. It's OK.'

'I feel such an idiot. I never twigged about Jacy and Hélène. I just assumed he was English. I never knew he was French.'

'It's understandable. He's both! He was brought up in France but his dad's English and wanted him to have an English education apparently.'

'But "J-C", Jean-Claude! It's so obvious. And I knew Hélène was going out with a French courier, but as far as I was concerned, Jacy was an English courier – and I never saw him with a girl. I probably wouldn't have looked twice at him if I'd known he was French!'

'No change there, then!'

'Actually, I have changed over this holiday, you know I have. And of course I would have looked at him – he's divine – I just wouldn't have fancied my chances. And certainly not against Hélène! Ooooh, Mark. I feel so-o-o stupid. I really was in love with him, you know. At least, I thought I was. I've never had such gut-wrenching feelings about anyone before.'

'It hurts, doesn't it?'

'Yup.'

We sat in companionable silence for a while, both concerned with our own thoughts. Mark said, 'I want a tell you something complicated, Sophie. Complicated. Will ya hear me out?'

'OK.'

'It might embarrass you, but don't let it.'

'I could hardly be more embarrassed, could I?'

'I'm a big ugly bloke, me—'

'No you're n—'

'I said hear me out, and don't patronise me.'

'Sorry.'

'I'm big and clumsy and I don't have a particularly pretty face. Maybe I'll improve with age – that's what Emma says! But with girls I've always felt sure I was goin' a be rejected, so I sort of got round it by going for truly beautiful girls who I knew would put me down, like. I was going down the same road with you. You are very beautiful, as you well know, and, true to form, you were fairly unpleasant to me.'

'I know. Mark, I'm sorry.'

'No, wait. I haven't finished. Because since the barbecue you've behaved like a normal human being to me. A normal human being. We met on mutual territory. You knew I wasn't much to look at and I knew you could be a cow. But we've gone beyond that. We can stand to be with each other – and that's something new for me, Sophie. Something new. I'm in the company of a beautiful woman and she's not putting me down, making me feel like an ugly bloke. An ugly bloke.'

It was true. I didn't notice how he looked any more. I didn't notice how he spoke. I just saw the kindness and the hurt. He didn't notice how I looked any more either. It was as if I'd forfeited that when I was so bitchy to him. 'I don't see an ugly bloke at all, Mark. I see someone who is kind, with nice eyes.'

'Stop! Stop! You'll make me blush. I wasn't askin' for compliments.'

'And you saw someone who was unkind, with horrible scornful eyes.'

'I didn't say that, Sophie. And I think we ought to stop this conversation. I was only trying a tell you that you've been good for me.'

Now this isn't going to turn into a fairy tale, Beauty and the Beast and all that. I didn't suddenly kiss him or anything. I still didn't fancy him, and he knew that. But some day, when his spots have cleared up and he's lost a bit of weight, both of which will happen, he'll be a brilliant boyfriend for someone – someone nicer than me. I suddenly felt incredibly tired, and hungry. 'Do you think the disco's over yet?'

'It's only ten o'clock. You can come back to our tent if you like. Mam will no doubt have passed out and the boys might be asleep too. We can go round the bottom if you want to avoid people.'

'I do. I don't really even want to see Becky. She

hadn't put two and two together about Jacy and Hélène either.'

'Too immersed in her own affairs, probably. And it didn't affect her personally.'

'What about my brother and Emma? Did they know?'

'Well, of course they knew about Jacy and Hélène. Emma was referring to Hélène when she upset you so much. But they wouldn't have known that you were actually going to make a play for him.'

'I suppose only Becky knew that.'

'For anyone remotely interested it was probably common knowledge. Jacy spends half his time in the bar. They took yesterday off together. They sang together in the Karaoke.'

'With my parents, no less. Don't. It's all too humiliating.'

We walked up the other way to the tents. I could hear Mum and Dad talking, but they didn't see me. 'I'll go back when they've gone to bed.'

'Fine. What would you like to eat? I could knock you up a quick fried egg.'

'Perfect.' It was, too. That fried egg with French bread and butter was one of the nicest meals I've ever eaten. 'Just what the doctor ordered.'

'Maybe in ten years' time it will be!'

'I'd like to see you in ten years' time.'

'Let's not get carried away, now!'

'Perhaps my brother will marry your sister.'

'I wonder where they are?'

'I expect they'll all go down to the lake after the disco.'

'Are you quite sure you don't want to go?'

'Quite sure. I just want to hide away.'

'Would you mind if I went down there?'

'Of course not. If everyone's down there I can nip into the shower block without being seen and get into bed before Dan gets back. Mark, you won't tell people what happened to me, will you?'

'Now why would I do a thing like that? Plenty of people saw you when you'd fainted, but it was quite a crush back there and I think Fergal and me were the only ones who saw you when – you know. I'll just say it was too hot, and your ankle was hurting or something.'

'Tell Becky to come and see me in the morning – please?'

'You know I'm a pushover, me.'

I would have given him a kiss then for being such a lovely guy, but I was afraid he'd read too much into it. I promised myself I would before we went our separate ways, though. I so much wanted to make it up to him.

I fell asleep almost instantly – I was exhausted. But when I woke up the moon was shining brightly. It was still the middle of the night. I lay there, my brain totally alert, turning through everything that had happened. How could I have been so blind? So many little things fell into place once I was in possession of two simple facts: Jacy was French; Jacy was going out with Hélène. And it was as if, as soon as I'd seen them together and made the connection, I stopped being in love with him.

I had a lot to learn about love. If I'd really loved him, would I have accepted them being together quite so easily? There was no doubt my emotions had been in turmoil. The truth was, chasing Jacy had been a whole new experience for me. I was experiencing all those turbulent feelings for the first time. I had discovered, perhaps, a little of how Ben must have felt, or Mark, or even – and here I hardly wanted to admit the truth to myself because it made me feel so bad – Fergal.

I had behaved abominably to several people on this holiday, but to none of them more so than Fergal. I had toyed with his affections and used him. All right, I thought he knew he was part of a ploy, but that didn't excuse everything. That night by the bonfire – it had been wonderful being so close. If only . . . if only . . . And he was such a great guy – 'awesome' was Becky's word. I could have had him, but I'd let him slip away. I'd sent him away. He'd gone.

I found I was crying, for Jacy and for Fergal. I'd see Jacy in the morning, but he would be someone different – Jean-Claude, Frenchman, boyfriend of Hélène. I woudn't see Fergal in the morning. I'd never see him again. I sat up suddenly. Perhaps he hadn't gone yet. I'd never get him back but I could at least say sorry. I shone the torch on my watch – 3.30 a.m. They wouldn't have left yet! I quickly reached for a biro and a postcard and wrote: 'Fergal, please forgive me. I was blind. Write to me.' And I put my address. I could put it under the windscreen wiper of their camper van.

I unzipped my compartment and climbed out into the night. The moon was huge and beautiful. It was completely quiet. I slipped into my flip-flops and made my way up to the main path that went past the Acceuil. I was going to go down to their tents but then I realised that they would have to come this way when they left. I sat on the fence to wait for them, I didn't care how long for. And then I heard two cars, one of them the distinctive putt-putt of a VW. They would have to stop and lift the chain that went across the road. I stood there clutching my postcard. They seemed to take for ever, crawling up through the wood, but at last the two cars reached the chain. It was Fergal who climbed out to unhitch it. 'Fergal!' I whispered. He looked over in my direction. I went to him and gave him the card. I thought he wasn't going to take it at first. But he did. He read it without looking at me. Then he contemplated me sorrowfully for a few moments. 'Ah, Sophie,' he said at last. 'We mustn't regret what could have been.' The others drove through and waited for him to put the chain back. Gus knocked on the window to hurry him up. 'But I left a little poem for you on your car. I wrote it for you.' He never said goodbye but quickly took my hand and kissed it before jumping into the van and putt-putting into the distance, leaving me, a solitary waving figure under the moon.

I sat on the fence again for a few minutes. I felt so bereft. It was as though a limb had been amputated, so acutely painful was my sense of loss. I went back to the tent. I saw the piece of paper under our windscreen wiper. When had he put it there? The moon was bright enough to read by. Here is Fergal's poem:

Eyes from Heaven

You shine
like a woman in love.

Truly
I feel
my way,
direct all my meditation

on you

Knowing, even as I do
that your love is not for me.

That other woman
I lost
in the moment of my birth
must have shone
as you do

Shone with love for me
if only for that moment.

But her light
has dwindled,
lies low,
overwinters, waiting to be rekindled
and blossom into
flames again

by a woman who burns
with love for me alone.

Oh Fergal.

Fifteen

For the third time on this holiday I felt like an invalid.
Certainly my heart ached. I still felt like an amputee.
Danny knew I'd fainted but he was considerate enough
not to pass on this information to Mum and Dad. Mark
had been as good as his word – he hadn't told anyone,
not even Emma, what I'd been doing when I keeled
over.

Jacy was totally upfront about the whole affair. He
came over and told Mum and Dad he wanted to talk to me
about something, and then walked me over to the Aire
des Jeux as if we were discussing a football match. He was
very apologetic and said he was really really sorry if he'd
led me on. It was just that, since he'd known from his files
that I was fourteen before he even met me, and since
there was no secret about his relationship with Hélène, it
never occurred to him that I might take his jokes and
teasing seriously. He said it would make him more careful

in future and ended by saying – 'No hard feelings?' And I was able to answer truthfully – 'No, none.' Maybe I should have said I was sorry too, but I didn't think of that until later, and I didn't want to go any deeper or make it difficult to see him during our last few days. When we got back to our tent he double-checked with the parents that we'd be leaving on the Sunday and added that a family from our part of the world was stopping over on their way to the ferry on Friday night. He couldn't remember their names offhand, but their postcode was similar to ours.

Becky came over next. 'Come for a walk down to the lake,' she said, and tactfully asked no questions until we were on the path through the wood. 'I saw Jacy and Hélène together,' she said sympathetically. '*Why* didn't we make the connection earlier? It was so obvious!'

'I know,' I said. 'I couldn't believe I hadn't noticed. But it makes sense of everything, doesn't it?'

'Do you want to tell me what happened?' Becky asked. 'I know you fainted. Were you just nervous? I remembered you hadn't eaten all day.'

So I told her. I told her how I'd got into such a state that in the end I'd literally thrown myself at Jacy, and talked gibberish at him.

'What did you say?'

'Well, I got all confused. I'd thought of all these things to say to him, but they got mixed up.'

'Go on, what did you say first?'

'You'll never believe this.' Those first words had suddenly come back to me. 'Promise you won't laugh?'

'Why should I?' said Becky.

'All right. I said, "I am a sunflower".'

'You said *what*?' I knew the telltale signs – Becky was beginning to heave and had trouble keeping her face under control.

'You heard.'

'Aaaaa ha-ha!' Becky was away. '"I am a sunflower!" You didn't, did you?' Her laughter was completely infectious.

By now even I was beginning to see the joke. 'I did! I said, "I am a sunflower!"' I was going to explain to her about him being the sun, but I was too overcome with giggles. Becky doubled up and had to totter through the gap and sit down at the side of the empty tennis courts. I joined her, and together we rolled around on the grass, our eyes streaming, repeating over and over, when we could, 'I am a sunflower!'

'Becky, you are a tonic!' I told her when I had recovered temporarily. My gran used to say that about people and right now I knew just what she meant. I could so easily have spent the day feeling miserable. Trust Becky to make me see the funny side. The rest of what I'd said to Jacy was beginning to come back to me. 'Do you know what else I said to him? I was trying to say, "Dance with me", or "Kiss me", but I couldn't get the words out – so I ended up saying "Dance me!"' We were off again.

It was wonderful to be able to laugh at it all. I don't think I've ever laughed at myself quite like that before. I didn't mention the Fergal stuff to Becky. That really wasn't funny. I put it away somewhere in my head to think about later.

'What shall we do today?' asked Becky. 'It's early for us. Why don't we break the mould and do things differently for a change. I'm getting bored with the sleep/pool/bar/lake routine.'

'You mean, the sleep/pool/snog/bar/snog/lake/snog routine.'

'No, I don't mind the snogging bit! Dad's starting to ask a few too many questions, though. And I love being with John, but Steve and Suzette are beginning to get on my nerves.'

'Becky!' She'd said all this in her mild-mannered, light voice. 'We could go for a bike ride? Pick blackberries?'

'Brilliant!' she said, turning round to go back. 'We could go along the road to that place where we crossed with the horses. It's not far. I'll get Mum to do us a picnic.'

So that's what we did. It was almost as if the holiday had already ended. We went for a swim after supper instead of going to the bar and played boules with her parents until the light faded and then went to the bar where Becky's dad bought us Bleu Tropiques and my parents joined us along with Mary and our Dutch neighbours. We did sneak off a bit before they did so Becky could find John. As long as I didn't think about Fergal I was happy.

On Friday we played crazy golf in the morning and helped Coralie to organise a treasure hunt for the kids in the afternoon. But somehow after supper we drifted back to the bar. The others greeted us like old friends. I felt as though I'd been away. My brother and Emma were very much an item. Suzette and Steve, as Becky had said, were joined at the hip. They still couldn't understand a word the other said, but that didn't seem to bother them.

Jacy popped his head round the bar. 'Hi Sophie!' he said, in precisely the same way as he always had done, you know – friendly, helpful, the good courier. 'Those new people I was telling you about. They're called Southwell. Mean anything to you?' I nearly fell off my seat.

'Do they have a son called Ben?'

Jacy looked at a sheet of paper he was holding. 'Benjamin, age fourteen – that one?'

I couldn't believe it. Of all the campsites, of all the families – Ben had to turn up here. I think the gods have it in for me. 'Yes, the very same.'

'So you know them! Shall I tell them you're here, or do you want to surprise them? They're in the Acceuil at the moment – I'm about to take them to their tent. They're only here for one night.'

'Where is their tent?'

'Right down on the prairie.'

'Don't tell them. I'll go over there with Becky later. Thanks.'

'It's up to you. I won't say anything. Bye!'

'What's all this?' Becky had only half heard our conversation.

'Someone, a boy, I know from home, has just arrived at this campsite.'

'Really? Let's go and see him. Is he goodlooking?'

'Cool it, Becks.'

'Yeah, cool it, Becks,' said John and turned back to talk to Steve.

'It couldn't be worse. Something else to embarrass me. He's called Ben and we had this embarrassing scene at the end of term when he told me he was madly in love with me – and cried, and stuff.' I looked down. Now of course I felt ashamed of how unkindly I'd treated Ben, but him turning up here did seem particularly unfair.

'Jacy said they're only here for a night. It would be easy to avoid them altogether,' said Becky. She looked at John's back that was still turned on her. He hadn't been best pleased by us taking off these last two days. 'On the other hand, I bet he is goodlooking if he thought he had a chance with you, and I'd like to meet him. Wouldn't it be great to see the look of surprise on his face? Oh come on –' she was really getting into this now – 'we could take him down to the lake, show him what's what.'

'He's only here for one night.'

'All the more reason. Please?'

Maybe she was right. And I was going to have to face up to him next term. And I do like him – just not drooping around after me.

'OK. I've changed my mind. Let's go and find him.'

'Me and Sophie are just going to go and check out this old mate of hers,' said Becky to John. 'See you down at the bonfire?'

'Fine,' said John, and carried on talking.

'What's up with him?' I asked her as we set off for the prairie.

'Oh, I don't know. I think we both probably feel that this isn't going to go on after the holiday has finished, so what's the point.'

'But you live in Chester and he lives in Liverpool – they're quite close aren't they?'

'Ooh, you are learning! Yes, they are close but – not close enough.'

'Becky!'

'Oh, don't worry! We've had a good time. I expect we'll write for a bit, even meet up once or twice. But that's the good thing about a holiday romance isn't it? It can end with the holiday.'

'Or the bad thing.'

'I'm a realist, me. I don't honestly think I'm going to end up marrying John! We've had fun and that's it. Now, show me this Ben! The people left that tent over there this morning.'

I approached cautiously. A family was unloading stuff from a car. 'Ben!' called the mother. 'Take this to Dad would you?' The boy came out from the tent to the car. It was Ben.

'Wow!' said Becky from where we stood, mostly hidden by someone's four-wheel drive. 'You turned *him* down?'

Ben is my age but he's quite grown-up looking. He plays basketball for the school, so he's tall and fit. He had also acquired an astonishing tan, which we could judge for ourselves since he was wearing nothing but a pair of swimming shorts. He has ordinary brown hair normally, but now it was streaky from the sun. Three weeks in the south of France had done that.

'Introduce me!' said Becky.

'Shh,' I said. I felt shy all of a sudden. 'Don't forget he probably hates my guts.'

'Nah!' said Becky, giggling. Ben looked over in our direction and I'm ashamed to say we both ducked down behind the four-wheeler.

'This is ridiculous!' I said. 'We can hardly show our faces now!'

'We'll just have to crawl away,' said Becky, and started to do just that.

We heard the mum saying, 'Thanks Ben. Do you want to go and find some other young people now? Camilla can stay behind with us.' We stayed crouching to listen.

'I don't know,' said Ben. We couldn't see him. 'It's not the same without Rosie. And we're going home tomorrow.'

'Up to you, love. I just thought you might want to enjoy your last night before we go back to real life again.'

'Thanks for reminding me, Mum.'

'Well, you were in a bit of a state when we came away, darling,' she said.

'Becky!' I said, horrified. 'Help me!'

'Keep on crawling,' she whispered. 'We can go to our caravilla.' So we crawled, ignoring the curious glances we got from the other campers and ran for the row of caravillas as soon as we could.

'Who is Rosie?' she asked as soon as we'd thrown ourselves on to the seat.

'I don't know. A girl he met on his last campsite, presumably.'

'And was he in a state before they went away because of you?'

'Yes.'

'Hmmm. I know what. I'm going to wander by and say hi. I'm going to ask where he's from. And when he tells me, I'm going to ask if he knows you by any chance. And then I'll bring him over to you. We've got to give the poor guy a good last night. Don't you think? You won't have to say much down at the lake, just let him mix in.'

'Oh all right then. I'll go back to the bar.'

'Tell John I've gone to the loo or something. What d'you bet me I can get Ben over in under ten minutes?'

'A Bleu Tropique.'

So that's how I came to spend my second-to-last evening with Ben Southwell. He was quite cool at first, but then we got more friendly as we sat by the bonfire. We went out in a pedalo and sat back to chat as we pedalled together.

'So how've you been?' he asked.

'Not so bad,' I said noncommittally. I mean, I wasn't about to say that I'd made a complete idiot of myself over a courier and behaved badly towards the most amazing guy I've ever met, was I?

'You're looking good,' he said. 'Have you had all the boys falling at your feet as usual?'

'You don't look so bad yourself,' I said back. 'And have you had all the girls falling at your feet?'

'Just one in particular,' he said, and a faraway look came into his eyes.

'Oh yes?'

'She's called Rosie. And don't worry, Sophie, I'm over you now. I'm sorry about all that stuff at the end of term. I was very screwed up.'

I wasn't sure I wanted him to be so positive he was over me.

'Maybe next term will be different?' I said, smiling up at him, thinking how fit he looked, and wondering why I hadn't noticed before.

'Of course it will. I'll have Rosie. She doesn't live that far away.'

'Oh.' I felt ridiculously disappointed.

'Now introduce me to these friends of yours. Becky seems a laugh. It's my last night away and I want to have FUN!'

Ben's family left early next morning. I couldn't believe it was our last day. I spent most of it exchanging addresses. As it was a Saturday lots of new families were arriving. I saw them peering out of their car windows as they drove up the hill, watching all the activity that went on along the top, the human traffic that passed back and forth along that road. The couriers were frantically busy. The whole place was humming.

Becky stayed with me all day. John had accused her of flirting with Ben, which of course she had been, so it seemed as if their relationship really would end with the holiday. I felt slightly disillusioned – they'd been so good together! Becky had her own cynical explanation. 'It was almost as if he was doing me a favour, going out with me. As soon as I stopped being grateful he was less interested.'

'Oh Becky, that's not how it seemed to me. I think he really liked you. I think he was scared of you dumping him, so he decided to act cool first.'

'That's a very complicated explanation.'

'Trust me. I've been observing you. Enviously most of the time. And believe me, that guy really rates you. And he was right to think you'd be the first to get bored. Wasn't he?'

'I suppose that's true. OK, I'll be nice to him until we leave. It won't hurt, will it? After all, I'm going to be lonely when you go.'

Emma and Mark, John, Steve and Becky were all leaving on Monday, but it was most of our friends' last Saturday night. We decided to take over the crêperie, about fifteen of us, and have a meal together. Mum and Dad were very amused at such a sedate entertainment, but then they didn't see us dancing on the tables or any of the other things that went on.

My brother and Emma were glued to each other. Sweet lovers parting! You'd think they were married and he was going off to war or something! Mark and I had a laugh about our new in-law relationship.

'I still think that you and I will be the ones seeing each other in ten years, Mark, not them.'

'Aw shucks!'

'No, really, Mark. I think you're great. You're really special to me.'

'I'm blushing!'

'Now I'm going to do this once and once only, so you'd better prepare yourself.'

'What? What?' He looked at me all wide-eyed.

'This—' I reached across the table and gave him a great big smacker on the lips.

'Yay!' Everyone cheered as Mark sat back looking stunned. It was the cue for everyone to start kissing each other – it was our last night after all, and we wandered back to the tents together in a big group, loath to separate and say our final goodbyes.

'What time are you leaving?' asked Becky from where she was wrapped around John.

'About half-past eight.'

'I'll get up specially to say goodbye then!' Our other friends said that they would too. It was nice to think we were so popular.

The car was packed. Mum and Dad were getting our passports and signing off at the Acceuil. Danny and I were surrounded by a big crowd of bleary teenagers come to wave us off. Danny was awfully subdued when he finally said goodbye to Emma, and got in the car looking pink.

I was about to get in my side when Jacy appeared on his bicycle. 'Hi Sophie,' he said. 'Now, I'm being the good courier wishing you a safe journey and hoping you had a happy holiday, but I also want to give you the address where Hélène and I will be in Paris next term. It would be nice to hear from you if you felt like writing to your French friends sometimes.' He gave my arm a little squeeze. Of course it was dead sexy, but he was being friendly and kind. 'I mean it,' he said. And I believed him. I believed that despite all my silly attempts to impress him he quite liked the person underneath. 'A bientot!' he said, and cycled off. I got into the car and waved like crazy to Becky and all my friends, particularly Mark, who had a big brotherly arm around his tearful little sister.

Epilogue

Mum couldn't get over how quiet Dan and I were on the way home. Barely any squabbling or complaining – a record. We went on the overnight ferry, so the whole journey took an age, but it was a necessary journey for me, bridging the gap between two worlds, a time to reflect. We arrived home while it was still early in the morning. Mum made us take our own bags in but let us off the unpacking and sent us up to bed like small children.

When I tottered downstairs in the afternoon Mum said that Hannah had rung to remind me about the sleepover tonight – it was going to be at her house. A good thing, considering the chaos here, though I was quite surprised. Hannah tends to stay as far away from home and her parents as possible. We usually have the sleepovers in my loft. The sleepover! I was hit with the full significance of this particular sleepover as I unpacked and sorted my things out. Our holiday romances! What on earth was I going to say? What if they'd all managed to have one – even Charlotte – and I hadn't? Especially after my postcards.

Stay cool, Sophie. Stay cool. I did sort of have a romance with Fergal. Well, we kissed. Twice. I could have had a romance with Fergal. But I blew that one, didn't I? Perhaps I should just merge the Fergal and Jacy stories? No one would know. Fergal and Jacy. Fergal – the stars. Jacy – the sun. I winced all over again at the memory of 'I am a sunflower . . .' But it made me giggle too. There was nothing for it. I was going to have to tell the truth about Jacy as one big joke. Play for laughs. Maybe the others would be pleasantly surprised by this not-quite-so-cool Sophie. I'd keep quiet about Fergal though. It's not an episode I'm proud of.

It would be great to see the others. Suddenly I couldn't wait. No friends like old friends, eh? I had a shower and washed my hair and then put on the clothes that showed off my tan to best advantage (of course).

As I stepped out into the street I was struck by how autumnal it seemed – especially for someone wearing short shorts. Hannah's house is just round the corner from mine. I looked up and saw Maddy about to cross the road. Brilliant! 'Maddy!' I screamed at her, and waved like a lunatic. She waved back and skipped alarmingly through the traffic to my side of the road.

It was so good to give Maddy a hug and be enveloped in her latest scent. We compared tans. Hers was pretty amazing considering she's been home a while. Still, we can't all go to Barbados.

Neither of us knew where to begin. Maddy told me that not only had Hannah got herself a boyfriend on her music course – she was still going out with him! Secretly I think we were *both rather impressed. Charlotte hadn't told Maddy much about what happened in the Lake District, but she can be a quiet one. Then Maddy admitted that she had met someone gorgeous in Barbados, and I decided that I could certainly say in all honesty that I'd met someone gorgeous in France.*

We rang on Hannah's doorbell. I was really longing to see her again. I expect that some time I'll probably tell her the whole story about Jacy and how it felt to be in love with someone who wasn't the slightest bit interested in me, for a change. One day I might tell her about Fergal too, and even about Ben Southwell. But not tonight.

Also in the *GIRLS LIKE YOU QUARTET*:

Four girls, four lives, one summer.

It was Maddy's idea that all four of them should have holiday romances and report back at the end of the summer.

These are their stories . . .

Hannah

Hannah is the clever one, and hard to please – but she's really shy too. She doesn't fancy her chances on a summer music course – so she decides that the boys are just not worth bothering about . . . not any of them . . . or are they?

Maddy

Finding romance has never been a problem for Maddy – she's always been a beauty and dramatic with it. So she can't wait for her exotic holiday in Barbados with Dad – it's going to be brilliant, and so different from life at home with impoverished Mum. The stage is set – but is romance all that lies in store for Maddy?

Charlotte

Shy, dreamy Charlotte has been going to the Lake District every year for as long as she can remember and she's loved Josh from afar for as long. But this year she's going without her older sister. It might be the chance she's been waiting for. What if Josh notices her. Just because she's four years younger than him – it doesn't mean all her dreams won't come true – does it?